GLADIATOR SCHOOL
BOOK 2

BLOOD & FIRE

DAN SCOTT

SCRIBO
A division of Book House

First published in Great Britain by Scribo MMXIII
Scribo, a division of Book House, an imprint of
The Salariya Book Company
25 Marlborough Place, Brighton, BN1 1UB
www.salariya.com

ISBN 978-1-908973-60-3

The right of Dan Scott to be identified as the author of this work has been asserted
in accordance with sections 77 and 78 of the Copyright, Designs
and Patents Act, 1988.

Book Design by David Salariya

Special thanks to Rachel Moss

Condition of Sale
This book is sold subject to the condition that it shall not, by way of trade or
otherwise, be lent, re-sold, hired out or otherwise circulated without the publisher's
prior consent in any form, binding or cover other than that in which it is published
and without a similar condition being imposed on the subsequent purchaser.

Printed and bound in India.
Reprinted in MMXV.

The text for this book is set in Cochin
The display type is P22 Durer Caps

www.scribobooks.com

GLADIATOR SCHOOL
BOOK 2

BLOOD & FIRE

DAN SCOTT

SCRIBO

A division of Book House

Mount Vesuvius

House of M. Nemonius Valens

Vesuvius Gate

To Rome

To the Harbour

Forum

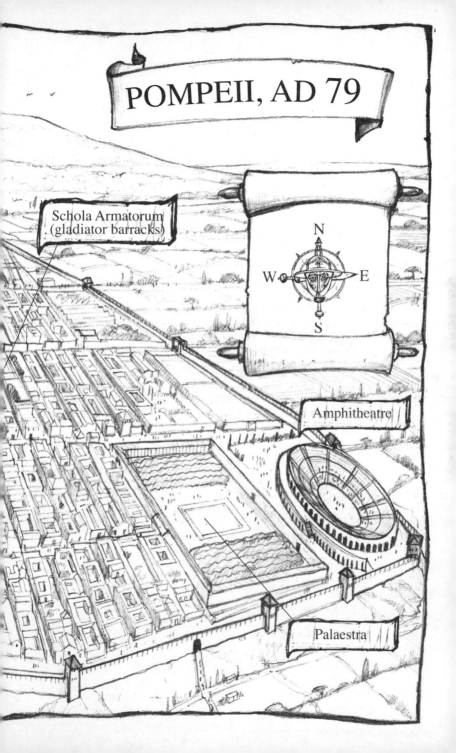

POMPEII, AD 79

Schola Armatorum (gladiator barracks)

N
W — E
S

Amphitheatre

Palaestra

Blood Oath Selected by Julia Eccleshare
March 2013 Debut of the Month
lovereading4kids.co.uk

Introducing Gladiator School, a series of novels set in a rich and textured world of dusty arenas, heated battles, fierce loyalty and fiercer rivalry. Follow young Lucius as his privileged life is suddenly turned upside down, leading him to seek answers amongst the slaves and warriors who work and train at Rome's gladiator school.

What the lovereading4kids reader reviews say about *Blood Oath*:

'The beginning of this book really gripped me so I would not put it down.'
GRACE PARKER, AGE 10

'I loved this book because it has some action and mystery makes it a really exciting story. It's brilliant; it has a mix of different genres so it is suitable for everyone. You will love it!!!'
CHRISTOPHER TANNER, AGE 11

'I also liked this book because every time I read it, it made me feel like I was actually in Ancient Rome with Lucius and sometimes I would look up from this book and be surprised to find myself in my bedroom!'
LUCY MINTON, AGE 9

'There is only one single bad thing about this book and that is that it ends!'
ADAM GRAHAM, AGE 9

'This novel was really compelling, I just couldn't set it down! I also liked the way it told you what the Roman word meant in English – it was really interesting.'
CARLA McGUIGAN, AGE 12

'The gladiators' fights were really exciting and sometimes I wasn't sure if they would live or die. If you like adventures with a touch of mystery you will love this book.'
SAM HARPER, AGE 9

'I enjoyed this book because I was sitting on the edge of my seat wondering what was going to happen next.'
SHAKRIST MASUPHAN-BOODLE, AGE 10

THE MAIN CHARACTERS

Lucius, a Roman boy

Quintus, his older brother

Aquila, their father

Ravilla, their uncle

Caecilia, their mother

Valeria, their sister

Isidora, Lucius's friend, an Egyptian slave

Crassus, a lanista (trainer of gladiators)

Valens, editor (sponsor) of the games
at Pompeii

Atia, a seer

Eprius, a young patrician (nobleman)
of Pompeii

FIRST BLOOD

ROME
10 AUGUST AD 79

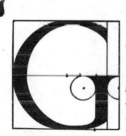ames given by Gaius Valerius Ravilla,' Lucius read aloud. 'Forty gladiators will fight. Perfumed water will be scattered.' His finger hovered over his brother's name. 'Quintus, Retiarius, tiro, will battle Burbo, Secutor.* Burbo has won ten bouts.'

'You've read it at least twenty times,' said Isidora, sounding rather impatient. 'You can't change the words by staring at them, you know.'

Lucius dropped the programme back into his bag and rubbed his eyes. He hadn't had much sleep.

---

* *Retiarius: a gladiator who fights with net (rete) and trident; tiro: a gladiator fighting in public for the first time. Secutor: a gladiator who wears an enclosed, egg-shaped helmet and fights with a short sword (gladius); his name means 'Chaser'.*

'He should be battling another tiro, not a veteranus* with ten victory palms,' he said.

'It shows how talented he is, that they've matched him with someone like that,' Isidora said. 'Thanks to you he has a good chance – now you have to leave the rest up to him.'

Lucius knew that she was right, but it was easier said than done.

They had squeezed themselves into the hot corridor among the cages again, this time with permission to watch a couple of matches before going back to the school. It was obvious from the arena floor that there had already been several gory fights, and the crowd's lust for death was growing. The air was rank with sweat and blood.

Lucius looked across the amphitheatre at the Emperor Titus, who was leaning back and laughing with Ravilla. He wondered if Titus knew that one of the gladiators he was about to watch was the sponsor's nephew.

Quin and his opponent, Burbo, were already in the arena doing their warm-up exercises. Burbo had a few supporters calling his name, but the crowd loved an underdog and there were just as many people shouting Quin's name and wishing him luck.

There was a hush as the musicians signalled the start of the battle, and then a sense of anticipation as Quin circled around the heavily armoured Secutor,

---

* *veteranus: a trained fighter who has survived at least one combat.*

feinting with his net. Burbo raised his sword and Quin jabbed at his leg with the trident. Burbo deflected it with his shield and sprang towards Quin, who darted backwards. There was a roar of approval from the crowd – it was a good start.

Circling again, Quin shook his net playfully across the sand, taunting his opponent. Burbo charged at him but he sprang aside, casting the net as he leapt. The Secutor avoided the net and charged at Quin again, but Quin could run faster than anyone Lucius knew.

He breathed a sigh of temporary relief as the heavily armoured Secutor chased his brother around the arena. Burbo had no chance of catching him. Quin's advantage was speed and lightness – Burbo would tire out far more quickly.

After several minutes, Quin drew nearer to Burbo again, staying at trident's length. He started to circle him faster and faster, making Burbo turn on the spot to keep him in sight.

'He's trying to make him dizzy,' said Lucius, clenching his fists. 'Come on, Quin, faster!'

As if they had heard him, the crowd took up the chant – 'Faster! Faster!'

Quin threw his net and lunged with his trident at the same time. But Burbo's experience showed and he avoided them both, slashing at Quin's back with his gladius.* Quin arched quickly away from him, but not quite quickly enough. The gladius drew a long,

---

* gladius: short sword; the standard Roman infantry sword.

shallow cut across his back and bright-red blood trickled down. The crowd howled in delight.

'First blood to Burbo!' they yelled. 'Come on, Burbo!'

Lucius could tell from the way his brother's chin jerked upwards that Quin was annoyed to have been the first to be cut.

'Keep your temper,' he muttered under his breath. 'Stay focused.'

Quin slammed his trident into Burbo's leg so fast and hard that the Secutor went down with an almighty crash. The crowd erupted, but Burbo was on his feet again in an instant – the bronze greave on his leg had protected him.

Burbo stamped on the net that was lying on the sand and slashed at it with his gladius. Quin jerked the net from under Burbo's foot and sent him crashing to the ground, but he rolled sideways and scrambled to his feet again, hurling himself after Quin.

The battle ranged across the full breadth of the arena, giving everyone a chance to see the gladiators up close. When they neared the corridor where Lucius was squatting, he saw that they were both sweating and bleeding freely, but neither of them had a serious wound. This could take a long time. Lucius felt as if the inside of his skin was turning cold, despite the stifling heat.

Quin led Burbo back into the centre of the arena, every now and then flinging his net without letting it go, forcing the Secutor to jump over it like a child's skipping rope. The crowd screamed with mocking laughter.

'Dance, Chaser, dance!' they shouted.

Burbo was getting tired. The weight of his armour was gradually making him slower, and the crowd shouted louder still, sensing weakness.

'You've got him now, Quin!'

'Don't let him rest!'

'Make him chase you again!'

'Charge him!'

They were so loud that their shouts of advice to the fighting men reverberated inside Lucius's head. Burbo seemed to have heard them too, because he suddenly charged, his gladius up, and knocked Quin's trident from his hand. Burbo gave it a kick that sent it flying across the arena. Quin turned to run after it, but before he could get away, Burbo grabbed him by the tunic and hauled him backwards. Lucius cried out as the blade of the gladius flashed down, but Quin was ready. He threw his net over Burbo's head and gave a powerful tug on the mesh. Burbo stumbled and crashed to the sand.

Quin released his net as Burbo lumbered to his feet, and then flicked it towards Burbo's legs again. This time the Secutor's jump was too slow. The net whipped around his legs, throwing him down once more.

Faster than thought, Quin rushed forward, picked up his trident and used it to knock the sword out of

Burbo's hand. Burbo lunged after it, but his legs were still enmeshed. Quin stood over him, pointing the prongs of his trident at Burbo's throat.

Burbo's chest was heaving as he gasped for air and raised the index finger of his left hand.

'He's asking for mercy!' Lucius cried.

'Lucius has won!' shouted Isidora, jumping to her feet. 'Yes!'

Quin released Burbo from the net and the young Secutor knelt at his feet.

'Kill him!' shrieked the crowd. 'Kill him!'

'Spare him,' said Lucius, staring at his brother.

Isidora put her hand on his shoulder.

'It's the Emperor's decision today,' she said.

Please don't make him kill, Lucius thought. *Don't make him do that. Not today.*

Titus was quick to give his verdict. He stood up and held out his palm with the thumb covered. Lucius's bones seemed to turn to jelly.

'Mercy,' said Isidora. 'He must have thought that they both fought well.'

'Thank the gods,' said Lucius.

He looked at his uncle, whom he could just glimpse behind Titus's throne. Did Ravilla know that Lucius was watching him? He hoped so. He felt a sudden surge of wellbeing and self-belief. Anything seemed possible.

'Ravilla's got away with it so far, but one day I'm going to expose him for the cheat he is. But first I've got to find Father and clear his name.'

Isidora didn't reply. She seemed to be deep in thought. Quin was jogging around the arena with his first victory palm, waving to the crowd. They were screaming his name, and he looked reinvigorated. Titus was standing up, holding a metal plate that contained a pile of coins.

'Lucius, let's go,' said Isidora, tugging on his tunic.

'In a minute,' he replied. 'I want to see Quin get his prize.'

'No, listen, I've been thinking,' she said.

'It can wait for one minute!'

'Remember the wax tablet you found in the underground office?' she went on, as if he hadn't spoken. 'It didn't make any sense because we didn't know what it was about, but we do now. I think we should go back down there and take it!'

'We can't just take it!' said Lucius.

'Why not?' she demanded. 'Weren't you just saying that you want to expose him as a cheat? This could be the proof you need.'

'I didn't think you were actually *listening*,' said Lucius, grinning at her despite himself. 'Besides, I gave him my word not to say anything about the match fixing as long as he stopped it straight away.'

'Oh, yes, because you can always trust Ravilla to keep his promises,' said Isidora.

Twenty minutes later, Lucius was inside the underground office, with Isidora urging him to hurry up. The leather boxes were still empty apart from the wax tablet. He took it and stuffed it into his messenger bag, wishing that he didn't feel so guilty.

'It's like being at war,' he told himself aloud. 'Sometimes you have to do things you're not very proud of.'

'What did you say?' hissed Isidora from outside.

'Nothing.'

'What's taking you so long?' she asked, poking her head around the door. 'I don't like it down here.'

'It was your idea,' he said, stepping around the desk and picking up the lucerna.*

'Stop!' she exclaimed. 'What's that?'

She pointed at the floor beside the desk. Lucius peered down.

'I can't see anything.'

'I'm sure there was something – it must have been the way you were holding the light. Bring it lower.'

They crouched down and Isidora gave a cry of triumph and picked up a small roll of thin lead.

'What is it?' she asked.

Lucius took it and peered at it. It was dirty and had obviously been there for some time. It was pure luck that she had seen the light fall on the small, unmarked piece of metal.

---

* *lucerna: a Roman oil lamp, usually made of pottery, shaped like a bowl with a handle on one side and a spout on the other.*

'It's a curse tablet,' he said. 'My uncle must have dropped it without realising.'

'We have those in Egypt too,' Isidora commented. 'What does it say?'

'It's a *curse*, Isidora! I'm not going to *read* it!'

'Well *I* will, then,' she said, taking it back from him. 'I'm not scared of your gods.'

She carefully unrolled the soft tablet and held it close to the lamp while she read the words aloud.

*To you, ferryman and death-bringer Charon:**

I invoke your name in order that you help to hold back Aquila, to whom my mother gave birth, and turn his life to wretched darkness, shame and torment. Make him suffer and remove him from my presence, and let him meet his end in a bad way. Quickly, quickly!

'Let me see that!' said Lucius, snatching it from her.

He read the text through three times, his thoughts whirling. Then he looked up. The flickering light was making their shadows jump on the walls.

'Have the gods helped to shame my father?' he asked. 'How can I fight against their magic?'

'Shake yourself out of it, Lucius,' said Isidora in her most sensible voice. 'There's nothing divine about what happened to your father.'

---

* Charon: in Greek and Roman mythology, the ferryman who carries the souls of the dead across the River Styx to the underworld.

Lucius pushed past her and blundered back along the dark passageway. He didn't stop until he reached the top of the steps and could stand in the bright sunlight again. He took several deep breaths. There was something very unpleasant about that underground room. It made him feel panicky. Even now, its damp mustiness seemed to be clinging to him.

He walked across to the fountain and drank. Then he splashed water onto his face and combed it into his hair with his fingers. Isidora followed him and placed her hand on his arm.

'I'm sorry,' she said. 'Did I offend you?'

'No,' said Lucius. 'I just couldn't stay down there and think straight, that's all.'

'So you don't think that this was the "will of the gods"?' she asked, holding out the little lead tablet.

'No,' he said, taking it from her and looking down at it. 'All this curse proves is that my uncle wanted to get rid of my father. Maybe he managed it.'

'What do you mean?' she asked.

He looked up at her and felt a surge of hope.

'Don't you see?' he asked. 'Ravilla told me that he had helped Father to get away – but what if he was the one who denounced him in the first place?'

'Ravilla's capable of anything, I know that,' said Isidora. 'But I don't understand why you're looking so pleased about it.'

'Because if Ravilla was behind the denunciation, I think there's a good chance that he has the proof my father was looking for,' Lucius explained. 'Rufus said that I was the only one who could get it, and I didn't understand what he meant. But that would make sense if it's hidden in Ravilla's villa or something. I'm his family – I could get access. If I could find the proof it might not matter that I don't know where Father is.'

'That's a lot of ifs,' Isidora pointed out.

Lucius knew that she was right. Finding the proof his father needed was not going to be an easy task. But he had just watched his brother defeat a fully armed Secutor while wearing little more than a loincloth. Today, anything seemed possible.

After the musty darkness of the underground office, the warmth of the sun seemed to give him strength. It was as if the gods were telling him that he had the power to turn his fortunes around.

'Ravilla's behind what's happened to us, I know it,' he said. 'And somewhere there is bound to be evidence of what he's done.'

Isidora stared at him, and then gave a little nod. Lucius knew that she would do all she could to help. He filled two of the fountain cups and handed one to her. Then he raised the other.

'Here's to friendship,' he said.

'To friendship,' she replied.

He lifted his chin and straightened his back. Strength and certainty were surging through him. One day he would prove his father's innocence. In the meantime, he had a friend he could trust with his life. He had a brother who was the hero of the gladiator school. These were riches – greater riches than he had ever understood before.

Whatever the future held, Lucius was ready to face it.

But before Lucius could continue with his search for the truth, there came an unwelcome announcement: a troupe of gladiators from the school was being sent to take part in a festival of games in the seaside town of Pompeii, a whole week's march to the south – and Lucius would be joining them…

PART ONE

PROPHECY

CHAPTER I

POMPEII
19 AUGUST AD 79

120 hours before the eruption of Vesuvius

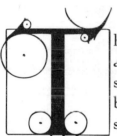he midday sun beat down on Lucius as he pursued Quin through the streets of Pompeii. He glimpsed his brother's tall, athletic figure up ahead, sauntering along through the crowds heading west towards the Forum.* Lucius would have preferred to walk side by side with Quin through this unfamiliar city, but sensed he would not be welcomed.

Smells of cooking meat from the fast-food shops mingled with the stench wafting over from the fish-sauce factories near the harbour. Lucius's ears echoed with the cries of fruit sellers and wine merchants and the pipes and drums of buskers. The noise and

* Forum: the main marketplace, which was also the place for business meetings and political discussions.

squalor reminded him of Suburra, the area where he now lived in Rome. Yet Pompeii seemed to carry an extra air of menace. The shadow-filled alleys, the hard faces of the young men, the cold-eyed stare of a beggar woman – they all spelled danger to Lucius. Maybe it was his imagination, but Pompeii seemed like a city brimming with desperate and unscrupulous people who'd murder you for the price of a loaf of bread. He was glad he'd decided to follow Quin. Somehow, he felt his brother needed watching in a place like this. Of course, Quin was a gladiator and very capable of looking after himself – yet Lucius knew he could be hot-headed at times, and in these strange and scary streets he might very easily get himself into trouble.

From a nearby side street, Lucius heard a cry of pain. His natural caution made him want to hurry on past, but then he saw Quin turn and enter the alley. Hesitantly, Lucius followed, rubbing the ring on his forefinger for luck. It was his only memento of his father, and had become his talisman. Concealing himself behind a pile of amphorae,* Lucius saw Quin approach a group of rough-looking young men. They were jeering and pushing around a lad of about their own age. From his smart, formal toga, now bespattered with mud, Lucius could tell the victim was a young man of status, though this did not seem to count for much among his tormentors.

* amphorae (singular amphora): earthenware storage jars.

His sense of fairness clearly offended, Quin impulsively strode into the mêlée and pushed aside one of the bullies, who had been holding the victim in a neck lock. The bully squealed in surprise and fell to the ground. His friends immediately closed in around Quin, their jeers turning to snarls of anger.

There were six of them – three armed with sticks – against the unarmed Quin. Lucius groaned. He steeled himself, knowing he would have to go and help his brother. With his slender build, Lucius wasn't made for physical violence. He cursed their fate for bringing them here to Pompeii.

It was ten days since Crassus, the lanista of the gladiator school, had made the announcement. The school had received a great honour, he said: it had been chosen to represent Rome at the forthcoming games in Pompeii. A total of thirty gladiators would be going, including Quin. And Lucius had been dismayed to learn that he too was among those selected to go. It was a seven-day march to Pompeii, and there would be a further week spent in the city. Taking the return march into account, that meant that Lucius would be gone from Rome for three whole weeks – time he had been hoping to spend searching for his father. What if Aquila tried to contact him during that time? It seemed that fate had once again intervened to prevent them from meeting.

Lucius was surprised to have been chosen. Surely there would be slaves at the gladiators' quarters in Pompeii; what did they need him for? Equally baffling was Quin's inclusion in the party. He may have recently fought and won his first combat in the arena, making him a veteranus, yet he remained one of the least experienced gladiators at the school. It almost seemed as if Ravilla wanted to get both Lucius and Quin away from Rome. He had probably sensed Lucius's growing suspicions of him, but why send Quin? Ravilla had always seemed on very friendly terms with him.

It had been a tough march from Rome to Pompeii – especially for Lucius, who wasn't used to travelling such distances on foot. Being less valuable than the gladiators, he was also given smaller rations for the journey. As well as suffering from hunger and exhaustion, Lucius felt lonely. Quin mingled with his fellow gladiators during the rest stops and in the evenings, but Lucius was excluded from their banter. He was sad that the changes in their family circumstances had driven him and Quin apart. He'd never been best friends with his brother, but he remembered times when they'd had fun together. Nowadays, Quin was focused only on his new 'familia' at the gladiator school, and seemed to have almost forgotten that he had a real family as well. Lucius, however, could not stop thinking about his family. As they marched along the dusty road, he occupied the hours wondering where his father might be, or hoping that his mother and sister would remain safe without him or Quin around. He wished many times that Isidora could be with him. He really missed her cheerful presence.

By the sixth day, they had reached the beautiful sweep of the Bay of Neapolis.* The sun sparkled on the blue sea as they marched through the pretty resort towns of Baiae, Puteoli, Neapolis and Herculaneum, with their white-walled villas and pink-tiled roofs. Friendly faces clapped and cheered as they passed.

Looming ever closer as they continued east was the brooding bulk of Mount Vesuvius, its cone-shaped summit wreathed in smoke. Lucius remembered reading of this mountain in Strabo's *Geography*. The Greek scholar had described it as having rocks at its summit that looked as though they had been 'eaten out by fire'. The mountain was certainly much bigger than he had expected, and dominated their horizon for most of the final day's march.

On the morning of the seventh day, the gladiator troupe arrived in Pompeii. The crowds were out to welcome them, but they struck Lucius as a cruder, less respectful populace than those in other towns they'd passed through. A few catcalls could be heard among the cheers, and there were some mocking salutes. A group of young women giggled as the gladiators passed them. Young boys stared open-mouthed at the bulging muscles on display.

---

* *Neapolis: present-day Naples.*

Several of the buildings they passed were covered in scaffolding. Lucius had once read in his father's library that Pompeii was practically a new town after its virtual destruction in an earthquake seventeen years earlier. Many people had arrived in the years since to make their fortunes here, putting up new buildings to replace the damaged ones and then renting them out. They had become the new elite, displacing the old moneyed families that had been Pompeii's original inhabitants. Lucius remembered Aquila telling him that Pompeii had become a wilder, rougher place since the earthquake, almost like a frontier town on the edge of the empire.

The troupe soon arrived at the Schola Armatorum, the gladiator barracks where they would be quartered during their stay in Pompeii. It looked like a new, post-earthquake building, its outer walls freshly decorated with colourful frescoes of gladiators in combat. They were greeted at the entrance by the manager of the Schola, a tall, thin man by the name of Gaius Calidius. He showed them around the spacious interior of the building, which included a training arena, a weapons room, a trophy room, a communal dining area and a space for relaxation, as well as dormitories.

Several dormitories were already occupied by gladiators who had arrived from other cities on the Italian peninsula. Calidius told them that five troupes in total would be competing in the games, and it was all being generously sponsored by Marcus Nemonius

Valens, a wealthy businessman of high standing in Pompeii. It promised to be a spectacular event.

Lucius was quartered with the slaves who staffed the Schola Armatorum. He decided not to tell them that he wasn't actually a slave himself, fearful that this might cause resentment. In his simple brown tunic, caked in dust after his long journey, he supposed he must have been indistinguishable from a slave anyway. It would have greatly surprised his dormitory mates to learn that just weeks ago he'd been living a life of luxury, with slaves of his own. Lucius could scarcely believe it himself. His old life was rapidly taking on the quality of a dream.

After he had washed and changed, Lucius went off to find Quin to check that he had a decent place to sleep. He found him in the atrium talking with Crassus. Quin was asking the lanista for permission to go out and look around the city. To Lucius's surprise, Crassus agreed. And so it was that Quin stepped out into the sunlit street and Lucius decided, on impulse, to follow him...

Now Lucius wished he'd tried to stop Quin from ever venturing out into these savage streets. They should have stayed in the safety of the Schola Armatorum, or at least waited until they could be guided to the safer areas by a trusted local. He watched despairingly as the youths closed in around Quin. Lying dazed on the floor of the alley was the well-attired young man Quin had tried to save. Lucius saw the bullies raise their sticks high above their heads and draw back their legs to kick his brother. How could Lucius help? He wasn't a fighter!

As the first blows began to land on Quin, Lucius gritted his teeth, trying to muster up some courage to join the fray. Before he could, there came a sudden explosion of movement from Quin. One of the bullies went flying backwards, another was sent spinning into a wall, while a third was tossed head over heels, landing in a groaning heap near where Lucius was hiding. One of the remaining boys, deciding that he'd met his match, fled down the alley. Two, however, remained. The bigger of them – more man than boy – spread his arms wide. In his right fist, a knife blade glinted. He advanced on Quin and thrust the knife towards his chest. Quin darted out of reach, and in the same movement kicked the knife out of the young man's hand. As he did so, he was clouted over the head by the other lad's stick. Quin's eyes glazed over. His legs wobbled, and he crashed to his knees.

Lucius had seen enough. He came charging out of his hiding place and ran at the younger boy from behind, pushing him. The boy staggered but remained on his feet. When he turned and saw Lucius's puny frame, his lips spread in a nasty grin. By now the bigger lad had retrieved his knife, and Lucius found himself facing not just one but two young Pompeiian street fighters.

He felt a heavy blow on his arm, but it came from neither of the two local lads. It came, instead, from Quin, who by now had staggered back to his feet and was glaring furiously at his younger brother. 'What are you doing here?' he hissed. He began grappling with the bigger of the bullies, but still seemed to have time and energy to make his feelings known to Lucius. 'Were you following me?'

'I'm sorry,' said Lucius, as he backed away from the other lad. 'I didn't want to leave you on your own in a strange city.' He leapt to one side as the boy's stick came crashing down, missing him by a whisker. 'Looks like I was right to be worried!'

Quin angrily forced the big Pompeiian youth onto his back. 'I know this city better than you think,' he spat.

'You've been here before?' asked Lucius, picking up a broken amphora and desperately hurling it at his assailant.

'I came here once on business,' Quin replied curtly, as he pinned his adversary to the ground.

'You mean with Father?'

Quin was so enraged by this question, he let go of the bully. 'You know, Ravilla's right about you!' he growled. 'You're nothing but a little sneak! Always spying on your betters!'

'Look out!' yelled Lucius.

Quin dodged as a knife blade brushed narrowly past his arm. But his moment of inattention cost him dearly. As Quin lunged to his left, his opponent pushed him further in that direction, wrenching himself around so that he was now on top of him, with his knife pressing into Quin's neck. At the same time the other boy forced Lucius onto his back and was now kneeling on his chest, stick raised high, ready to bring it crashing down on Lucius's skull.

Both Lucius and Quin had lost their fights – but this was not the arena. There would be no last-minute pleas from the crowd for clemency. All they could expect now was death – in a Pompeii side street, at the hands of a couple of thugs. What an ignominious ending to their lives!

Just then there came a low rumble that seemed to emerge from beneath the ground. The rumble became a violent shaking that Lucius felt deep within his bones. The pile of amphorae collapsed, shattering into a thousand clay shards. From above, roof tiles began to tumble. One of them hit the big Pompeiian lad on the head. Screams could be heard from the main thoroughfare, as clouds of pinkish-brown dust rose to fill the narrow alley.

Lucius coughed and choked on the dust. When the shaking stopped and the dust finally began to clear, he found his opponent had fled. The larger youth was lying unconscious on his side, a bloody gash across the top of his forehead. Behind him, Lucius heard footsteps receding. He turned in time to see his brother striding away down the alley towards the street.

'Quin!' he yelled, but Quin didn't break his stride. Soon he had disappeared around the corner.

Lucius slowly picked himself up.

'Thank you!' came a weak voice from the dusty shadows at the side of the alley.

Lucius peered towards the source of the voice. 'Who's there?'

As the dust continued to settle, he saw the figure of the boy who had been the original victim of the bullies.

'My name is Eprius,' said the boy, struggling to his feet. 'You and that other young man were very brave, coming to my aid like that.'

His toga was dirty and torn and there was blood on his cheek. Yet he had the accent and bearing of a person of noble rank.

'You're welcome,' said Lucius. 'I'm pleased you're all right. What was all that shaking just now?'

'An earthquake,' said Eprius. 'We're quite used to them here in Pompeii, although they have become more frequent and violent of late. The timing of this one was most fortuitous, wouldn't you agree?'

Lucius smiled and nodded. 'I'm Lucius,' he said. 'The other one was my brother, Quintus. Why were those boys picking on you?'

Eprius blushed and looked down at his sandals. 'I'd rather not say, if you don't mind. Perhaps I've strayed where I shouldn't – done a few things I wish I hadn't.

This city can be cruel, you know. It punishes those who cross the line, and it doesn't matter who you are.'

Lucius didn't know what to make of this strange speech, so he simply said: 'Well, I'm glad we could be of help.'

'I thank you, Lucius,' said Eprius. 'May the gods protect you and your brother during your stay in our city.' He nodded his farewell and limped back up the alley towards the main street.

Lucius was now alone. With a jolt, he realised that he had no idea how to get back to the Schola Armatorum. He was about to run after Eprius and ask him for directions, when he stopped. He felt a prickling of his neck hairs. Someone was watching him, he was sure of it. He surveyed the dim surroundings of the alley. The big Pompeiian youth still lay sprawled unconscious in the dust. Apart from him, no one was about.

Then he saw them, glinting up at him from the shadows: a pair of eyes.

Lucius couldn't move. He stared back at the eyes. Dark pinpricks surrounded by pools of silvery blue, beneath hooded lids, they seemed to bore right into him, fixing him to the spot.

Gradually, the owner of the eyes rose up from the shadows and emerged into the light. Lucius saw that it was just a little girl – a girl even younger than his sister Valeria. She was small, with a round, grubby face, tanned deep brown from a life spent on the streets. Dressed in rags, with a dirty scarf wrapped around her head, she was nothing more than a waif, an urchin, perhaps seven years old – yet her eyes continued to mesmerise him. Bright, almost luminous blue within her brown face, they seemed ancient and full of mysterious wisdom.

As Lucius stared back at her, the little girl raised her hand to the sky and began to shout strange words at him: 'I see darkness,' she said, 'a sky so black it blots out the sun. This shaking of the ground is just the start. I see terrible things coming out from the underworld. The doors of Hades* shall stand open and send forth fire and scalding winds. The sea shall swell and rage and foam. The clouds shall drip with burning fire.'

'What do you mean?' Lucius asked her.

'I see the end,' muttered the girl. 'The end of days. The end of everything!'

Just then there came the sound of approaching footsteps and voices echoing off the narrow walls. The girl looked startled and tried to shrink back into the shadows, but Lucius grabbed her arm.

'Are you a seer?' he asked her. He'd heard of people who claimed to see the future, but they were usually very old.

The girl tried to pull away from him, but Lucius held her tight. A group of friends appeared at the end of the alley, laughing and chattering. One of them, a young woman, noticed Lucius and the little girl.

_____

* *Hades: the Roman underworld, the abode of the dead.*

'Ah, look!' she cried. 'Atia's found a friend. I wouldn't touch her if I were you, stranger. She's nothing but a street urchin, and she only ever has one thing to sell – doom.'

'You know her?' Lucius asked the woman, still holding on to the girl.

'Oh, everyone who lives around here knows Atia,' laughed the woman. 'And everyone knows she's crazy. If you want prophecies, there are plenty of genuine, adult seers in the town.' She looked at the girl. 'Go home, Atia – if you have one – and leave the young man alone.'

Lucius released his hold on the girl and she melted back into the shadows. The woman rejoined her friends and they continued on their way, their laughter, like the twittering of birds, gradually fading away.

Once again, Lucius found himself alone in the alleyway. He wondered if he should try to find Atia. He was intrigued by her words, and wanted to know more. But then he heard more footsteps, and Quin reappeared.

'I suppose I can't very well leave you alone in this city.' he said to Lucius. 'Come along then, little brother!' He turned about and began marching back up the alley. Lucius, greatly relieved, trotted along after him.

'Please tell me why you came here before,' Lucius asked once he'd caught up with him.

'None of your business,' said Quin, increasing his pace and forcing Lucius to break, once again, into a jog. The two of them continued back to the Schola Armatorum in silence.

CHAPTER II

20 AUGUST

100 hours before the eruption

y the next morning, Lucius had managed to put Atia out of his mind. Instead, as he helped serve up a breakfast of barley, boiled beans, oatmeal, raisins and ash to the gladiators, he was consumed with thoughts of his father. Could it be true that he had once come here, to Pompeii, on business? It made sense of his father's observations to him that Pompeii was like a wild frontier town. How could he have known that except through personal experience? And if he did come here, then perhaps there were clues somewhere that could lead Lucius to him. He wished he could ask Quin what exactly their business had been in Pompeii. But Quin always became furious whenever he asked

such questions. Besides, his brother had already finished his breakfast and was now in the training arena practising his moves. Lucius wondered what Isidora would advise him to do. She was always full of ideas. If only she could be here with him, he wouldn't feel half so miserable or alone.

After he'd had his own breakfast, Lucius went to find Crassus to receive his instructions for the day. Crassus was in the training arena, busy tutoring a Thracian gladiator on the finer points of fighting with a curved sword, and a quarter of an hour went by before Lucius could capture the lanista's attention.

'I'm sure there's plenty you can do, Lucius,' said Crassus impatiently. 'But I can't think about that right now. The games are starting tomorrow and I've got to get these men into shape. I'll send you your orders shortly. In the meantime, why don't you ask the slaves if you can help with anything?'

So Lucius went to see Piso, the head slave. Piso looked him up and down and shook his head dismissively. 'I've got nothing for you. Go and see the cook.'

It turned out that Lucius was not needed by the cook, nor by the slaves in charge of cleaning or maintenance. Frustrated and bored, he retired to the dormitory and lay on his bed. If he'd been back at the villa, he would have spent this time in his father's library, reading about philosophy or history. He recalled the dry smell of the papyrus scrolls as he opened them to reveal beautifully written texts and exciting new worlds of knowledge and ideas. Now his father's books had been sold, and there were strangers sitting in his library.

An hour crawled by and the promised orders from Crassus failed to materialise, so Lucius decided to remind him of his presence by returning to the training hall. The gladiators were gleaming with sweat by now as Crassus pushed them through their routines again and again. He spotted Quin making sweeping motions with his net and jabs with his trident at a shield and dummy suspended from a swinging pole. After each strike of the shield, he had to step smartly to one side to avoid the heavy sandbag attached to the rotating pole as it swung back towards him. The catlike reflexes he had developed from this exercise had probably saved his life against the big Pompeiian boy the day before.

Eventually, Crassus spotted Lucius sitting on a bench at the edge of the arena. The lanista frowned, and at first Lucius thought he must be angry, but then he realised that Crassus was deep in thought. After a moment, Crassus beckoned to him. Lucius followed him to a room adjoining the arena. The room, which was lined with shelves containing spare gladiatorial equipment, also contained a table, a chair and some writing materials. Crassus wiped the arena dust from his hands and seated himself at the table. He took a piece of plain papyrus* from the top of a pile, dipped

---

* papyrus: paper made from an Egyptian reed.

a reed pen into a bronze inkpot and began to write. Lucius peered over the lanista's broad shoulder. In his shaky, rather uncertain hand, Crassus was writing a simple message of greetings and respect to the local worthy who had paid for the games.

When he had finished, he rolled up the papyrus, tied a ribbon around it and handed it to Lucius. 'Take this to Marcus Nemonius Valens,' he instructed. 'Make sure you hand it to him personally.'

'Why personally?' asked Lucius.

Crassus sighed and leaned back in his chair. 'I've invested a lot of hours and sweat on that bunch out there,' he said, nodding towards the door that led back into the arena. 'Your uncle has invested something even more precious – his money. We know nothing about this Valens character. This is the first games he's sponsored. I want you to look the man in the eyes as you hand him the message – try and see what kind of man he is. Cruel or humane? The kind of man who'll be merciful to my gladiators if they lose a bout – or the kind who'll think nothing of ordering their deaths if the crowd demands it? Take a look at his slaves while you're there, in his house. You can always judge a man by his slaves. Do they look happy? Sad? Frightened? I'll be waiting for your report with interest.'

Lucius stared at him. 'You want me to be your spy.'

'Apparently you have a talent for it,' smirked Crassus '– according to your brother.' He laughed. 'I guess it must run in the family!'

This was not the first time Crassus had mocked Lucius about his father and his alleged career as an informer. Lucius felt his face heating up. He clenched his fists to keep himself under control. If he spoke his feelings now, it could easily cost him his job.

'Where does Valens live?' he asked stiffly. He would do as Crassus wanted. After all, it would be interesting to meet the man who might end up deciding Quin's fate.

'In a large house in the north of the city, near the Vesuvius Gate,' answered Crassus. 'Ask for directions when you get to the Forum. Anyone will be able to tell you. He's one of the richest men in Pompeii.'

In the oldest area of the city, around the Forum, the streets were narrow and crooked. The roads were clogged with animal dung, rotting vegetables and other rubbish. Overflowing water from the city's fountains and drains turned the roads into filthy rivers, making Lucius grateful for the high pavements and stepping-stone road crossings. But these couldn't protect him from the overpowering smells of sweat and manure, not to mention the stale human urine that was used in the city's laundries to clean and bleach the citizens' smart white togas.

The city seemed caught up in election fever, and the Forum was filled with supporters of various candidates

for the offices of aedile and duovir,* all trying to
out-shout each other. The walls of houses and shop
fronts were daubed with election slogans in red and
black paint:

MARCUS HOLCONIUS PRISCUS
FOR DUOVIR!

I ASK YOU TO ELECT GAIUS JULIUS
POLYBIUS. HE BAKES GOOD BREAD

ALL THE LATE-NIGHT DRINKERS ASK YOU
TO VOTE FOR MARCUS CERRINUS VATIA
FOR AEDILE

THE PETTY THIEVES SUPPORT VATIA
FOR AEDILE

As before, Lucius felt nervous and vulnerable as he
passed through the agitated, sweating crowds. He
sensed malevolent eyes upon him, sizing him up,
making preparations to attack. A beggar's dog barked
loudly at him, making him jump. Once or twice, in the
gloomier alleyways, he thought he glimpsed the street
urchin, Atia, peering up at him from the shadows.

The street sloped upwards quite steeply as he
walked north from the Forum, and Lucius was hot

* *aedile: a junior official responsible for organising festivals and maintaining
public order; duovir: one of a pair of senior officials, with various duties.*

and tired by the time he arrived at Valens's house. The entrance was simply a door placed between two shops – a jeweller's and a shoe shop. The door, however, was massive: three metres high and bronze-studded.

Lucius knocked, wondering if his feeble raps would even be heard above the street noises. But the door was soon opened by a tall, well-muscled porter wearing a green tunic with a red belt. He looked down his nose at Lucius. With his blond hair and pale complexion, Lucius guessed he must be of Germanic origin.

'What do you want?' the porter asked.

Lucius held out the scroll. 'My master, Appius Seius Crassus, wishes me to convey this message to Marcus Nemonius Valens.'

'I'll see he gets it,' said the porter, holding out a broad palm.

'I was told I must hand it to him personally,' said Lucius, trying hard not to be overawed by the man's size and fierce look.

'Let him in, Marcipor,' came a soft voice from within.

The porter stood aside and Lucius entered. The door closed behind him, cutting off the sounds of the street. He found himself in a corridor, not much wider than the door. The air was cool and scented with roses. From somewhere in the house, Lucius could hear the faint chirruping of tropical birds.

Another man, dressed in a spotless white tunic, now stood before him – the household steward, Lucius assumed. 'Am I right in saying that you have a message for my master?' he asked politely.

Lucius nodded. 'Yes. From the lanista of the gladiator school in Rome.'

'Then I am sure my master will be only too pleased to receive it from you. Please follow me,' said the steward.

Lucius was led down the corridor towards the atrium. A couple of young male slaves, aged no more than twelve, were coming in the other direction. They eyed Lucius curiously as they passed. Sunlight poured through the square opening in the roof of the atrium, gleaming on the colourful mosaic floor and dappling the surface of the shallow pool that dominated the centre of the room.

'Please wait here,' said the steward, and he passed through a curtained exit at the far end. Lucius glimpsed another room beyond – the tablinum, with its tables and chairs, where the master of the house would receive his clients* and conduct his business.

He sat down on one of the long, marble seats by the pool and glanced at his surroundings. The atrium walls were decorated with frescoes of scenes from Greek mythology. Fresh flowers and fruit had been laid on the household altar, set into one of the walls. Lucius couldn't help but be reminded of the similar shrine in his family's old villa. They had taken their

---

* *clients: people dependent on a higher-ranking person for favours; hangers-on.*

lares – the small, carved figures representing their ancestor spirits – to the new flat, but it was sad to think that another family's lares were now occupying that once-sacred space.

Near the altar was a bust of a man on a marble plinth. The figure had a high, domed forehead and a mild, fleshy face – presumably this was Valens. He looked quite friendly, Lucius thought.

As he waited, three other boy slaves passed through the atrium, their sharp eyes darting in his direction as they went by. After five minutes, the steward returned and ushered Lucius through the curtain. Lucius followed him into the tablinum. This elegant room opened onto the peristyle, a colonnaded walkway that enclosed a rectangular garden of geometric flowerbeds bordered by neat hedges and footpaths. The flowerbeds were planted with cypress bushes, roses, artemisia and pinks. In the centre was a marble fountain. How luxurious to have this beautiful, secluded space in the middle of a bustling town. Valens had to be a very rich man indeed!

The peaceful atmosphere, with its gentle soundtrack of birdsong, was suddenly interrupted by a loud, very deep roar that made Lucius stiffen.

'What was that?' he gasped.

'Oh, nothing to worry about,' smiled the steward. 'The master keeps a small menagerie of wild animals – exotic beasts from Africa. That's where we'll find him now, in fact.'

On the far side of the garden, they crossed a marble-floored space with a number of doors leading off it. From behind one of these doors, Lucius could hear echoing splashes and laughter – the sounds of a private bath-house. Another slave, no older than Lucius, appeared suddenly, forcing Lucius to stop in his tracks to avoid a collision. The youth was bearing a tray containing a flask of body oil and a strigil – a curved blade for scraping off sweat and dirt. The boy flashed him a look of irritation, and for a moment Lucius thought he recognised him as one of the bullies from the day before – but, before he could be sure, the slave had entered the bath-house and disappeared into a cloud of steam.

The steward led him through a pair of tall black gates into an open area filled with iron cages, with narrow brick paths running between them. Out here, the sound of the birds, which Lucius had found quite soothing earlier, had risen greatly in volume and was now about as restful as the traffic in Rome on a festival day. He flinched from the noise, and also from the powerful animal odour coming from the cages.

The first creature he saw was a huge black bear. It was standing on its hind legs, snout pressed close to the bars; its thick paws, ending in long, sharp claws, poked through. It eyed Lucius as he warily followed the steward along one of the paths. As they walked, Lucius encountered several creatures which he recognised only from paintings and mosaics; others, like the giant bird with the long neck and tiny head, he had never seen before. Equally new to Lucius was a black-and-white striped horse. In the tallest cage he saw a creature with brown patches on its coat and an immensely long neck. There was a cage of monkeys clambering over the branches of a dead tree, and an aviary with parrots, peacocks, finches and blackbirds, all squawking and chirruping at the tops of their voices. As Lucius took all this in, the air was split once again by a roar – this time uncomfortably close.

'Feeding time for the lion,' remarked the steward cheerfully.

They rounded a corner and there it stood, less than three paces away. Lucius had seen paintings of lions on the walls of the gladiator school, but nothing could have prepared him for the ferocious reality of the maned beast. A slave was throwing chunks of red meat through the bars of its cage, and the lion was attacking these and devouring them savagely, almost angrily. Lucius stared, transfixed by the sight of its immense, black-lipped jaws; its teeth, sharp as spears, dripped with saliva as they ripped into the flesh. He shuddered as he recalled the stories of criminals and runaway slaves being thrown to the lions in the amphitheatre. Until this moment, the stories had meant little to him. Now, he couldn't help but imagine the horror felt by those wretches as they came face to face with such a ravenous monster in front of a crowd screaming for their blood.

'Impressive, wouldn't you agree?' came a mild voice to his rear.

Lucius turned. Standing there behind him was a short, plump man in his thirties, wearing a toga. Lucius immediately recognised him from the bust in the atrium – this was the master of the house, Marcus Nemonius Valens. Realising that his mouth was still dangling open, Lucius shut it with a snap, and nodded.

'Yes, very,' he croaked.

Valens looked past Lucius at the lion and said: 'We put carvings of these creatures on our tombs as symbols of death, but it seems to me that they are the very embodiment of life – life at its most vigorous and energetic!'

Lucius could only nod.

Valens smiled kindly at him, and Lucius couldn't help smiling back. He felt instantly at ease in the presence of this man.

'You have a message for me, I believe,' continued Valens, 'from the lanista of the famous ludus* in Rome, no less.'

Lucius handed over the scroll. Valens took it, then nodded at the steward and the animal feeder. The men bowed and withdrew.

'Come, let us leave this noble creature to his meal,' said Valens, and he beckoned Lucius to follow him. They left the growls and squawks of the menagerie

---

* *ludus: gladiator school.*

and passed through an interior walkway with a vaulted roof into a small, shaded courtyard. From one of its vine-draped walls, the sculpted face of the sea-god Neptune gushed water from its mouth into a pool.

'Take a seat,' said Valens, gesturing to one of the curved stone benches next to the fountain. Lucius did so, surprised that this important man was prepared to give so much of his time to a mere boy – a slave, as far as Valens knew.

Valens seated himself opposite Lucius and opened the scroll. After giving it a cursory read, he rolled it up and returned his attention to the messenger.

'You are not a slave, am I right?' said Valens.

'How can you know that?' gasped Lucius.

Valens chuckled. 'I pride myself on my observational skills,' he said. 'The moment I laid eyes on you, young man, I could see that you carry yourself like a citizen – like a patrician,* in fact. Your hands are soft – they don't look as though they've seen much manual labour. Young as you are, you look as though you're more used to giving orders than receiving them. And yet here you are, in the service of a lanista – of lowlier status even than a gladiator. There's a story here, I'm certain of it. I'd be honoured if you'd satisfy my curiosity and tell me a little about yourself.'

Lucius was reticent by nature. His instinct was always to keep quiet about his family's history. Yet there was something about this kindly man that

* *patrician: a member of the upper classes; an aristocrat.*

made Lucius want to open up to him. Valens's calm, grey eyes did not seem judgemental or mocking. His smile was honest and friendly, utterly unlike Ravilla's thin-lipped sneer. Here was someone he felt he could trust.

So Lucius told Valens the whole of his story, starting from the day his father disappeared and ending with their arrival in Pompeii. While he talked, a young slave came in and served them each a refreshing drink. Valens listened intently throughout, nodding occasionally, but saying little.

Lucius was careful to talk only about his family, not about the gladiator school. Part of him was tempted to tell Valens about Ravilla's match-fixing activities, as this might cause their troupe's disqualification from the games and a swift return to Rome – but he stopped himself, knowing that it might easily lose him his job. Neither did he tell Valens about Ravilla's hatred of Aquila, nor of his own suspicion that it was Ravilla who was behind the allegations against his father. Like it or not, Lucius and his family still needed Ravilla, and now was not the time to betray him. So he left the question of how his father originally came under suspicion as a mystery, and the death of Rufus in the arena he explained as an unfortunate accident.

When Lucius had finished, Valens stood up and began pacing the courtyard, deep in thought. Eventually he said: 'I knew your father, Lucius.'

'You did?' said Lucius in surprise.

'Yes, we've had dealings in the past. And this is why I find your version of events so persuasive. Having met Aquila, I find it very hard to believe he would ever betray his friends in such a way. I cannot accept that he could be the Spectre.'

Lucius's heart swelled with gratitude and relief when he heard this. 'I'm so glad to have met someone else who believes in my father, as I do,' he said. 'He told me that the proof of his innocence exists, and he needs me to get hold of it. But first I need to find him, so he can tell me where this proof is. Do you think he might be here in Pompeii?'

Valens shook his head. 'I know most of what goes on in this town. If Aquila were here, I'm sure I would have heard about it.'

'Would you mind my asking how you came to meet my father?'

'Not at all,' replied Valens. 'There was a case of political corruption in this town, about seven years ago – it was not the first nor the last that Pompeii has suffered. Rogues seem to be attracted to Pompeii like moths to a candle, I'm sorry to say. At that time there was still a lot of rebuilding going on following the earthquake. The aediles were accused of accepting bribes in return for awarding building contracts. Your father was serving as a praetor* in Rome in those days, and he was sent to Pompeii to

* *praetor: a senior official elected by the Senate.*

judge the case. I was a magistrate serving on the town council, and I worked with Aquila to bring the guilty men to justice. I learned then that he was a man of honour and integrity, and I have no reason to alter that view now.'

The steward reappeared. 'Sir, some of your clients are awaiting your presence in the tablinum. Shall I tell them you are coming?'

Valens glanced up. 'Yes, I shall be there presently. Thank you.'

When the steward had gone, Valens turned again to Lucius, who had risen to his feet, preparing to take his leave.

'Are they finding you lots to do at the Schola Armatorum?' he asked.

'To be honest, I feel like something of a spare part,' confessed Lucius. 'I'm starting to wonder why they ever brought me to Pompeii.'

'Well then, why don't you come and work for me while you're here?' suggested Valens. 'So long as Crassus doesn't mind, of course. I have to host a few banquets and parties over the coming days – mostly in honour of dignitaries from out of town who've come to attend the games. My staff could use an extra pair of hands to help serve the guests. What do you say?'

'Are you sure?' cried Lucius eagerly. He couldn't think of anywhere he'd rather spend his time while in Pompeii than here in this beautiful villa, working for Valens. And while he was serving food and beverages to the guests, he'd be in the perfect spot to pick up any snippets of news. Perhaps one of these important visitors might know something about his father.

'Of course I'm sure,' said Valens. 'Why don't you go back now and secure yourself a leave of absence from Crassus? All being well, you can report for duty to Servius, my steward, first thing tomorrow morning.'

'He wants you to work for *him*?' thundered Crassus, his giant fist crashing down on the table.

They were back in the little room next door to the practice arena, which Crassus had commandeered as a temporary office. From his red cheeks and crashing fist, Lucius at first assumed Crassus was in a rage. But then the lanista's weather-beaten face began creasing into laughter.

'That was a nifty piece of work, my boy!' he gasped. 'I send you there with a message of greeting and the man ends up offering you a job! What does he want you for? Fodder for his pet lion?'

'To help serve his guests at some banquets and parties.'

'Sounds like a cushy little number,' chuckled Crassus. 'Very well, you have my consent. I'll let your uncle know where you are when he arrives here tomorrow.'

'Thank you,' said Lucius, his heart thumping with joy. He was especially happy to be missing the arrival of Ravilla – the less time he spent around that odious man, the better. He was about to leave the room when Crassus stayed him with a gesture.

'Before you go, you were going to tell me what you thought of Valens. I assume you liked him. Do you think he'll be merciful with my gladiators?'

Lucius nodded. 'I don't think you'll have anything to fear from him.'

Crassus nodded. 'Good. Because I'm sure the rabble from this town will be baying for blood. And his slaves? How did they seem?'

'Happy,' replied Lucius. 'They all seemed quite…'

'Quite what?'

Lucius was about to say '…young,' but he stopped himself. Perhaps it *was* a little mysterious that Valens employed so many boys, but it was not a mystery he wished to share with Crassus. His loyalties had shifted, he realised: he was working for Valens now – at least for the duration of his stay in Pompeii – and the secrets of his new master's household were no business of the lanista's.

'Quite what?' repeated Crassus.

'Quite content.'

CHAPTER III

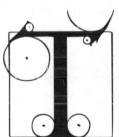

he following morning, Lucius returned to the house of Valens and reported to Servius, the steward. Servius escorted him to the atrium, then through another curtained exit in the opposite direction from the tablinum. As they walked, Servius pointed out the slaves' washroom, lavatory and dormitory, where he was told to deposit his small sack of personal belongings. This part of the house was very plain and gloomy, with low ceilings.

After passing a number of storerooms, they eventually arrived at the kitchen, where Lucius was introduced to the head cook, a large man with wild hair called Otho. Lucius was issued with a grubby apron and told to help with the preparations for the afternoon's banquet. The kitchen was dark, hot and filled with greasy smoke. The slaves working there seemed a cheerful crew, yelling jokes and banter at each other while working hard at their tasks – making pastry, grinding spices, stirring sauces in pots over a red-hot charcoal stove, or turning a huge boar on a spit over a fire. Otho set Lucius to work chopping parsnips, onion and garlic.

Every now and then there would be a delivery of fresh fish and seafood from the harbour, or meat and poultry from nearby farms. This was usually the cue for a general gossip, with the delivery man plied with questions by the kitchen slaves. During one of these interludes, Lucius learned that the Aqua Augusta, the aqueduct that supplied fresh water to the Bay of Neapolis, had mysteriously slowed to a trickle in some of the towns west of Pompeii. Dogs, cats and other animals had been seen that morning leaving Herculaneum, and farmers had reported seeing giants on the lower slopes of Vesuvius. These tales provoked laughter among the slaves, but Lucius listened with fascination. He was reminded of the strange prophecy he'd heard the previous day from that little girl, Atia.

The banquet began at hora duodecima,* as the sun was sinking across the Bay of Neapolis. Before commencing his serving duties, Lucius washed off

---

* *hora duodecima: the twelfth hour. The length of the Roman hour varied with the seasons, but the twelfth hour of the day was always the last hour of daylight.*

the grease and sweat of his labours in the kitchen and changed into a fresh white tunic. He and four other slaves entered the triclinium (dining room) bearing trays containing the first course: jellyfish and eggs; sea urchins with spices, oil and egg sauce; raw vegetables; sows' udders stuffed with milk and eggs; and boiled tree fungi with peppery fish sauce.

The room was long and narrow, with a row of windows at the far end, opening onto one side of the peristyle that Lucius had seen the day before. Three long couches were arranged in a U-shape around a row of low tables on which the food was placed. Valens reclined on the couch at the far end of the room, at the base of the U, giving him a good view of all his guests. He nodded and smiled at Lucius as he reached to take a sea urchin. Placed near Valens was a large, important-looking man with several chins. He was wearing a very shiny white toga – usually a sign of a man seeking public office. Two other men were engaged in a fierce argument, and the attention of the room was mostly fixed on them. One, whom the others called Crispus, had sharp, ratlike features and a narrow beard that jutted from his chin like the battering ram of a warship. He enjoyed stabbing the air with his finger as he made his points. The other, named Bellicianus, had a broad, red face and eyes that flashed with anger whenever the other man spoke.

Among the guests, Lucius counted just two women. He also spotted a young man, and with a shock of recognition he saw that this was Eprius, the youth he and Quin had saved from the bullies two days ago. The wound to his cheek was still visible as a thin dark line. Lucius had little chance to wonder what business the boy might have in such elevated company, for Servius was signalling to him from the doorway to return to the kitchen.

The next course had to be brought on in several stages. Otho, looking much cleaner now, and with his unruly hair neatly combed, accompanied the servers into the triclinium, where he proudly described each dish to the guests: milk-fattened snails in garlic; ostrich boiled with figs and bay leaves; dormice stuffed with pork and pine kernels in honey sauce; roast flamingo baked in a pastry crust. But the real showpiece was a wild boar whose belly seemed to shimmer and wobble as Lucius and another slave brought it out on its enormous platter.

'Is it alive?' one of the female guests asked nervously.

With a flourish, Otho plucked a large carving knife from his belt and proceeded to slice open the belly. To roars of surprise and delight from the couches, a small flock of thrushes flew out of the boar's stomach with a frenzied beating of their little wings. Lucius noticed Valens smile, as if satisfied with the reaction from his guests – it looked as though he'd seen this novelty dish before. The only guest not joining in the excitement was Eprius. He looked despondent, as if he'd rather be anywhere but here.

The frightened birds began wheeling crazily around the room, depositing little white droppings on the floor and – to Crispus's wild amusement – on Bellicianus's toga. Using brooms and mops, Lucius and the slaves attempted to coax the birds out of the windows at the far end. Meanwhile, Otho bowed and drank in the applause of the guests.

While Lucius was busy cleaning up after the birds, he felt Eprius's eyes on him. He looked up and smiled. The boy nodded briefly but did not return the smile. His plate, Lucius noted, was empty. The other guests were already grabbing snails and dormice or pieces of ostrich and feeding themselves greedily. Lucius tried to overhear their conversation.

Bellicianus was speaking to the man with many chins, who was reclining next to him: 'Priscus, my friend, I can certainly deliver you the votes you need. I have agents on the streets, and in the guilds – the laundrymen, bakers, fishermen and jewellers – they'll all vote the way I tell them. But you must promise me, in return, that when you are elected duovir, you will judge in my favour in my little disagreement with Crispus.'

'Bellicianus exaggerates his power, as usual,' said Crispus as he chewed on a snail. 'He controls two wards at most.'

'You are a liar, Crispus, and you know it!' bellowed Bellicianus. 'I got Cuspius Pansa elected as aedile last year, didn't I?'

'You were lucky!' replied Crispus dismissively. 'The opposition was feeble.' He turned to Priscus. 'If you want to be duovir, you must come to me. I control the most powerful guilds of Pompeii – the fullers, carpenters and fruit sellers, the goldsmiths and plumbers. And let's not forget the temples – Apollo, Isis and Jupiter. The worshippers will vote the way my agents tell them. I can set things in motion tomorrow, and in a few weeks you'll be sitting pretty as duovir. But first you must assure me that I can rely on a favourable verdict in my property dispute with Bellicianus.'

Lucius was shocked. So this was how politics worked in Pompeii! Businessmen got magistrates elected so that the magistrates would do as the businessmen wanted. Valens had not exaggerated when he told him that the town was rife with corruption.

Crispus and Bellicianus both eyed Priscus, each hoping for some sign of his favour, but Priscus looked more interested in his slice of flamingo pie than in either of them or their boasts.

'Friends, let's stop all this!' cried Valens good-humouredly. He gestured to an elderly man to his right, who had twinkling grey eyes. 'Our honoured guest Decimus Gallo didn't come all the way from Neapolis to hear us bickering about local politics, and neither did his esteemed wife Claudia.' He nodded at a lady of similar age, sharing Gallo's couch. 'Let us raise a toast to the new emperor,' said Valens. 'May his reign be long and glorious.'

'And low in taxes,' muttered Crispus.

The guests drank from their goblets of fine Falernian wine. Valens caught Lucius's eye and winked at him. 'Bring us some more wine, Lucius,' he murmured. 'And some bowls of water so we can rinse our hands.'

Lucius returned to the kitchen.

'What is going on with Bellicianus and Crispus?' he asked Mico, one of the kitchen slaves, as he filled a fresh flagon of wine from the barrel.

'Oh, those two are old enemies,' replied Mico. 'Between them, they own about half the tenement buildings in Pompeii. They bought up the land cheap after the earthquake, and then made themselves rich by building blocks of flats and renting them out. Trouble is, the earthquake also destroyed most of the public records about where one property ends and another begins, so Bellicianus and Crispus are forever fighting over this or that patch of land and who it belongs to. It's very entertaining for us lot, watching them go at one other's throats all the time, but I swear they'll kill each other one of these days.'

'And the sad-faced young man?' asked Lucius. 'Who is he?'

'That's Crispus's son. Wouldn't you be sad if you had a father like him?'

Lucius nodded absently. Eprius, with his round, handsome face and dark curls, looked nothing like his father, but a lot like the lady seated to Crispus's left. He was probably miserable because he had been forced to accompany his mother and father to a boring banquet.

Mico helped Lucius bring out the wine and bowls of water. Despite Valens's efforts to bring peace to the room, Bellicianus and Crispus were once again arguing fiercely. When Lucius handed Valens his bowl of water, the master of the house smiled and rolled his eyes as if to say, 'Help! What do I do?' Then an idea seemed to occur to him. He motioned Lucius to stay where he was. Then he called for the attention of all the diners.

'Friends,' he cried. 'Do any of you know of Quintus Valerius Aquila?'

Lucius started at the mention of his father's name.

'The senator who disappeared, you mean?' asked Priscus.

'The man they call the Spectre,' said Crispus's wife.

'The very one,' said Valens. 'Although whether or not he is the Spectre is as yet unproven. Does anyone have any idea where he might have got to?'

Lucius's skin prickled with anticipation. He became very still as he waited to hear what the guests had to say.

'I don't know where he is,' said Bellicianus, suppressing a belch, 'but the man is a villain and no mistake. I had a friend in Rome – remember Libanius? He once made some joke about Vespasian and his lowly background. Thanks to the Spectre, the emperor got to hear about it, and Libanius paid for his little joke with his life. I hope they catch Aquila soon. His sort make my skin crawl.'

'What makes you so sure Aquila is the Spectre?' asked Valens.

'Because he ran,' replied Bellicianus. 'If he was innocent, he should have stuck around and tried to clear his name.'

He was set up! Lucius wanted to shout. *He was framed by his accuser – by his own brother! What choice did he have?*

'I agree with Bellicianus,' said Priscus, dabbing grease from his mouth with a napkin. This unexpected declaration made Crispus look up, alarmed – the last thing he wanted was for Priscus to agree with Bellicianus about anything. 'I met Aquila once,' continued Priscus, 'and I must say I didn't care for the fellow. Not friendly at all.'

Lucius bristled inside, but didn't move a muscle as he stood near the wall, waiting to hear what Priscus had to say next.

'It was a few years ago now,' said Priscus, 'when I was a young man living in Rome, starting out on my political career, trying to curry favour with men of influence, as one must do. I was hoping to become quaestor* that year, and I thought Aquila might give me his support. To soften him up, I offered him tickets for the games. As a co-sponsor I had managed to

* *quaestor: an important official in charge of public money.*

procure excellent seats. Do you think he took me up on it?' Priscus squirmed at the memory.

'No, he didn't,' chuckled Valens. 'And you never became quaestor, did you, Priscus? – which is why you ended up in this little backwater, trying your luck as a provincial magistrate.'

'Not true!' said Priscus. 'I've always loved the sea. And I couldn't bear to waste any more of my time and energy sucking up to the likes of Aquila. It wasn't just that he turned me down that day, but he was so *rude* about it. He actually called the games "barbaric". Told me I ought to find better things to spend my money on – like the poor! "The poor can't vote!" I reminded him, but he didn't even smile. A most unpleasant character. I hope they catch him and crucify him.'

Lucius clenched his fists. Valens might have meant well, bringing up the subject of his father, but he wasn't sure he could bear much more of this slander.

'Hear, hear!' said Crispus, who seemed determined to position himself on Priscus's side in the debate – even if it meant having to agree with his nemesis, Bellicianus. 'I've never met the man personally, but I've heard people say he's a conceited old fool, with his head stuck permanently in a book. And his loathing of popular entertainment is well known. It doesn't surprise me that he turned out to be the Spectre. You have to be suspicious of anyone who doesn't enjoy good old-fashioned blood sports.'

'I'm not so sure,' said the elderly Decimus Gallo. 'Some of my friends used to be clients of Aquila, and they have all spoken well of him. He was, they say, generous with his time and always tried to help when he could. As a senator, I've heard, he worked tirelessly for the underprivileged in Rome. All right, so he didn't like the games. Not everyone does. He may have been more interested in books and learning than in the gory excitement of the arena. Is that a crime? I think not. We shouldn't be so quick to judge the man.'

Lucius inwardly cheered this speech. He decided he liked Decimus Gallo.

'So why did he flee then, eh, Gallo?' sneered Bellicianus. 'Answer me that!'

'I cannot,' said Gallo, bowing his head. 'All I will say is that there's a lot we don't know about this case, and we shouldn't leap to conclusions. He may return one day, who knows...' He turned to his wife. 'Claudia, my darling, did we not hear someone speak of Aquila at a party recently? Now what what was it he said?'

Claudia frowned, thinking to herself, while Lucius waited, scarcely daring to breathe in case he missed something.

'I think it was Gallio Flavianus, dear,' she said. 'A few weeks ago, he told us that Aquila had been seen in Herculaneum.'

Lucius stared at the lady. Herculaneum? That was a town just a few miles west of Pompeii, along the bay. They'd marched through it on their way here.

71

Claudia caught him staring, and frowned. Slaves should never stare and, as far as she knew, he was nothing more than a slave. Lucius hurriedly looked away, and as he did so his eye fell on the bowl of water in front of her. His mind in turmoil, it took him a few seconds to notice something odd about the water: its surface was vibrating.

How strange, thought Lucius. *Why should it do that?*

The following day, Valens asked Lucius to accompany him on his morning stroll around his little zoo. Happy and relaxed in his master's company, Lucius listened to his comments on the animals as he passed them.

'According to the learned naturalist Pliny,' remarked Valens, 'the elephant is the closest of all animals to humans in intelligence. It is frightened of rams and the squealing of pigs, and adores the smell of flowers and the sight of a beautiful woman. I can't say I've noticed any of this in our specimen here, but there you go – I'm not a natural philosopher.'

They stopped outside a cage containing a large pool of water. On the side of the pool a giant reptile with a long snout was sunning itself. Lucius stared in awe. 'Is that a *croc... croc-o-dile*?' he asked.

'All the way from the River Nile,' nodded Valens proudly. 'My sister uses its dung as a face whitener, would you believe?'

A tall Nubian slave named Tirano approached them with a bucket of fish.

'Cost me a small fortune to bring it over from Egypt,' said Valens. 'We needed a specially designed galley, complete with swimming pool. I tried bringing over a young hippo on the same trip. Big mistake.'

'What happened?'

'It ended up as this fellow's lunch.'

The creature was so still, Lucius thought it looked almost like a sculpture.

'It doesn't… *do* much, does it?' observed Lucius

Valens shrugged. 'Not much, no. But watch this.' He plucked a fish from Tirano's bucket and tossed it through the bars into the pool. At the sound of the splash, the reptile sprang to life. With a flick of its tail, it surged into the water and emerged a second later with the fish clamped in its jaws.

'There are not many creatures that can move faster,' said Valens with a chuckle. 'Except maybe Priscus when he attacked my snails at the banquet last night!'

Lucius laughed briefly, then frowned. The mention of Priscus reminded him of the nasty things he'd heard about his father.

Reading his thoughts, Valens said gently: 'Don't worry about what that old fool said. He's still bitter and twisted about never making it to the Senate, and he'll blame anyone he can think of for his failure – except himself, of course.'

Lucius nodded, grateful for these words.

'I'll send word to Herculaneum,' Valens told him. 'Maybe we'll hear some news of your father.'

'Thank you,' said Lucius, and tears of gratitude sprang to his eyes. 'You are very kind.'

'Don't mention it.'

Lucius looked at him, a single question burning inside his chest. 'Why are you doing all this for me?'

Valens continued to contemplate the crocodile for a while, before slowly turning to Lucius. 'Can you keep a secret?' he asked.

Lucius nodded.

'Then follow me.'

Valens led him out of the zoo and into the shaded courtyard. On the bench by the Neptune fountain, where Lucius had sat two days before, he saw a young man and woman seated next to each other. Putting his finger to his lips, Valens beckoned Lucius to join him in the shadow of a statue of Venus,* where they wouldn't be seen.

Lucius peered from behind the statue and saw that the young couple were holding hands. The boy, to his great surprise, was Eprius. He was wearing a tight smile, as if trying to appear cheerful, while murmuring something to the girl – but Lucius thought they both seemed rather sad and frustrated.

After a moment spent observing this scene, Lucius followed Valens back through the zoo and into the

* *Venus: the Roman goddess of love.*

lobby beyond. Two boy slaves were loitering near the bath-house entrance. When they saw Valens, they hurriedly moved on, sneaking a look at Lucius as they went and then exchanging glances.

Seemingly oblivious, Valens ushered Lucius through the lobby into the peristyle. They walked around the colonnaded walkway to an exedra – a semicircular recess, lined with benches. Valens sat down, spread his arms along the back of the bench and looked up at the half-dome ceiling, carved to resemble the interior of a seashell. 'The boy you saw out there in the courtyard is Eprius, son of Crispus,' he said.

Lucius, still standing, nodded, pretending innocence of this fact.

'The girl is Posilla, daughter of Bellicianus. As you probably gathered from yesterday's display, Crispus and Bellicianus hate each other. This is a tragedy for Eprius and Posilla. Their families are bitter enemies, so they cannot be together. But here they can meet, once a week, to talk.' Valens leaned forward and put his hands together between his knees. 'I'm a rich man, Lucius. And I wish to use my wealth for good. I like to help others when I can. That is why I'm helping Eprius and Posilla. And that is why I want to help you.'

CHAPTER IV

22 AUGUST

48 hours before the eruption

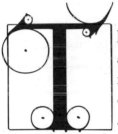he prisoner, escorted by two guards, staggered into the arena. He was naked but for a loincloth, and Lucius could see thick welts on his back from an earlier flogging. A wave of nausea washed through Lucius as the shouts and bellows from the crowd around him rose to a hysterical pitch. The guards tied the prisoner by his wrists and ankles to a stake near the centre of the arena. One of them used a dagger to open a fresh cut on his chest, then they departed. *The man is a murderer*, Lucius kept telling himself. *He deserves his fate.*

Lucius was sweating, despite the shade from the awning above him. As he stood there, on the dais, he tried to keep his face impassive, remembering he was visible to everyone. Seated immediately to his left was Valens, the editor* of the games. The dais was positioned halfway along the northern side of the oval amphitheatre, where the curve was flattest. Here, they were closest to the action – close enough to smell the blood.

When Valens had suggested that Lucius accompany him to the games as part of his personal retinue, Lucius had thanked him but said he'd rather not.

This had come as a surprise to Valens.

'Do you not wish to see your brother fight? He will be disappointed that you aren't there.'

When Valens put it like that, Lucius began to think that maybe he should go. Like it or not, Quin was now a gladiator, and it was Lucius's duty to support him. But he hadn't expected that he would also have to witness an execution!

Sensitive as ever to his feelings, Valens glanced at Lucius, then turned to the man on his left – Cuspius Pansa, one of the current aediles of Pompeii. Speaking loudly enough for Lucius to hear, he said: 'I find this quite abhorrent, don't you, Pansa?'

'Let's not forget that this man, Agorix, has murdered five people,' replied Pansa. 'He's a monster. And the people must have their justice.'

'Most assuredly,' agreed Gnaeus Helvius Sabinus, the town's other aedile, seated just behind them.

* *editor: sponsor or producer – the man who provided the money for the games.*

'At my temple they've been muttering that it's our soft attitude to justice that's displeasing the gods and causing all these earthquakes.'

Valens shrugged and raised his eyebrows at Lucius, as if to say 'You see my problem.'

The iron gates of the Porta Triumphalis, at the western end of the amphitheatre, slowly swung open and three lions emerged from the access tunnel into the dazzling sunlight. The beasts advanced hesitantly, keeping their bellies low to the sand-covered ground and their shoulder blades taut, as if intimidated by the feverish roars of the crowd around them. They looked malnourished, Lucius thought. He could see their ribs clearly beneath their pale gold fur, which was matted in places – nothing like the well-groomed, well-fed specimen in Valens's zoo. These animals must have been deliberately starved before the show.

The lions circled the perimeter, searching for a means of escape, but all they found was the sheer wall of polished stone that separated the arena from the first row of spectators. The gates at either end were now firmly closed. The capacity crowd, twenty thousand strong, yelled at the lions, demanding that they do what was expected of them.

In the middle, bound securely to his stake, the prisoner twisted his head fearfully from side to side, trying to see where his executioners were. When they appeared within his line of sight, his face seemed to turn the colour of wax and, for a few seconds, his body went rigid. Then he began frantically pulling at his bonds.

Eventually one of the lions picked up the scent of the man's blood, and probably his fear, and began closing in. Lucius shut his eyes and swallowed. As the excitement of the spectators grew, their roars and cries seemed to merge into a single howl of self-righteous hatred. Through half-closed eyelids, Lucius saw the lion just a few paces from the man, circling him, drawing closer with each pass. Its jaws were open and its teeth bared. The other two lions also began to approach, sensing the prospect of a meal. The prisoner's struggles with his ropes grew ever more desperate. He was crying with fear, though nothing could be heard from either him or the lions, such was the volume of the crowd.

Lucius didn't watch what happened next, but he sensed what was going on – far more clearly than he would have liked – from the changing noises of the mob around him. The fever of excited anticipation gave way to a strange sort of communal wailing as, he guessed, the first bite was taken. The sound faded, and in the sudden quiet he heard an unmistakable leonine roar. When the crowd found its voice again, it had fractured into a mosaic of thousands of individual cries, groans, shouts and yells – joined, this time, by deep-throated lion roars. Lucius squeezed his eyes shut, but he could do nothing to stop his imagination as he pictured the bloody feeding frenzy now taking place not a dozen paces from where he stood.

When the noises finally quietened, Lucius nervously reopened his eyes. The lions were gone and some men were dragging something from the arena – something attached to a broken stake. It took him a while to recognise it for what it had once been – a human being.

Fresh sand was soon thrown over the bloody patch in the centre of the arena, and Lucius wished he could obscure as easily the distressing sounds and images now etching themselves into his memory.

A fine, cooling mist of saffron-scented water filled the air around them, pumped through pipes concealed in the building's walls and sprayed from minute holes in the statues of the goddesses Fortuna, Mania and Victoria* at the rear of the podium.

'Oh, that's very pleasant!' gushed Sabinus.

It was lunchtime. Still dazed by what he had just witnessed, Lucius performed his duties, refilling Valens's goblet with wine and offering him an array of cold cuts, bread, cheese and dates.

'Go and get yourself a drink and a snack from a street vendor,' said Valens gently, pressing some coins into his palm. 'Stretch your legs. You look as though you need it.'

* *Fortuna, Mania and Victoria: the Roman goddesses of fortune (good or bad luck), the dead, and victory.*

Lucius thanked him and ran down the steps to the covered walkway that led to the amphitheatre's ceremonial entrance for use by the city's elite. The plaza outside was filled with stalls selling takeaway food, drinks and souvenirs. There were long queues of people buying refreshments for themselves or for their masters and mistresses. As he waited in line, Lucius scanned the posters on the amphitheatre wall. Some were announcing forthcoming gladiator fights, while others recorded results of recent bouts. He felt a twinge of sadness on seeing his brother's name written simply as Quintus Felix, with no mention of his family name, Valerius. Was this his way of denying his origins and taking on a new identity as part of the gladiator familia? Quin, he saw, was fighting this afternoon against a Secutor named Vibius Balbo – a local favourite according to some graffiti painted nearby: 'Vibius Balbo makes the girls swoon'.

After buying his drink, Lucius went and sat by a fountain. Try as he might, he couldn't clear his head of what he'd just witnessed. The worst part of it, in some ways, had been the crowd and its lust for blood. Now he understood more than ever why his father had called the games 'barbaric'. It seemed to make barbarians of even the most civilised people.

As he sat there with his drink, Lucius felt a prickling of the skin at the back of his neck, as if a cool breeze had swept in from somewhere. He knew this feeling – he was being watched. It didn't take him long to spot her, squatting on the pavement under the awning of a nearby tavern: Atia, the little street prophetess.

She came over to him, and once again he was struck by the amazing quality of her silvery-blue eyes – the wisdom and maturity that seemed to shine from them.

'They want to silence me,' she said to him.

'Who?' he asked dumbly.

She scooped some water from the fountain and drank. 'Everyone. They want to kill me. But the day I die, this city will die also.'

'How can you know that?' Lucius asked.

'I have seen it in my dreams. I have seen myself lying dead, while all around me our world is burning.'

'Your dreams may be wrong.'

She looked at him as a teacher might look upon a child. 'My dreams are never wrong,' she said simply. 'But if you don't believe me, look around you. The signs are everywhere, for those who have eyes to see them.' She pointed at the basin of the fountain. 'The level of the water is lower today than yesterday. Even the great Aqua Augusta is giving up on us. But no one wants to know.'

Lucius looked at the water. It did seem low, he had to admit. He noticed something else, too. Like the water in the bowl at yesterday's banquet, the surface of the water in the fountain was gently but quite noticeably vibrating.

'It will happen when I am killed,' she said calmly. 'And I will be killed very soon, I am certain of it.'

'Maybe I can help,' said Lucius, thinking of Valens and his generosity towards people in difficulty. 'Come with me.' He began walking towards the amphitheatre. Atia lingered by the fountain, staring at him. He held out his hand to her. After a moment, she followed him.

Back in the arena, the spectators were being treated to a comic interlude. Two musicians were performing, one playing the flute and dressed as a bear, the other playing the horn and dressed as a chicken. They were running around after a pair of paegniarii – mock gladiators – who were fighting each other with wooden swords. As each paegniarius landed a blow, the bear or the chicken would play a little tune – the more painful the strike, the more high-pitched and raucous the melody. The performance was provoking a lot of wild laughter, particularly from the uppermost tiers where the slaves and lower classes sat.

Valens was chatting with Pansa when Lucius returned with Atia in tow. During a lull in the conversation, Lucius cleared his throat and asked: 'Master, may I speak to you for a moment?'

'Of course,' said Valens, frowning slightly as his eye fell on the grubby little girl standing next to Lucius. In her rags and dirty headscarf, she looked decidedly out of place on the editor's podium.

'This girl is in danger,' Lucius explained. 'She says that people are trying to kill her, because... because of her warnings about...' He trailed off, realising how silly and childish he sounded.

'Her warnings about what?' prompted Valens.

'The end of days,' said Lucius, biting his lip.

Valens turned to Atia. 'What exactly do you mean, *the end of days*?' he asked.

'I have seen the future,' said Atia, turning her hypnotic eyes on him. 'I have seen how this city will die – in fire and in ash. The end of days is nigh. There will be darkness in the midst of the day. Pompeii will be destroyed – in fire and in ash.'

'When?' asked Valens, his mouth dry. 'When will this happen?'

Lucius was pleased, yet a little surprised, to see Valens taking the girl seriously. He wondered why he didn't shrug off her warnings, as everyone else did.

'It will happen,' said Atia. 'It will happen when I am killed.'

'Then we must keep you alive,' said Valens. He couldn't take his eyes off the girl, and Lucius was astonished to see him looking quite shaken. 'You shall stay in my house as my official augur,'* Valens told her. 'I can give you everything you need to make your visions clearer. Now what is it the sybils** use? I can give you birds, and cages full of snakes. Just let me know and I'll provide it.'

* *augur: a soothsayer who claimed to be able to interpret the will of the gods by observing natural phenomena such as the flight of birds or the entrails of sacrificed animals.*
** *sybils: female prophets.*

Atia shook her head. 'I do not see my visions in the flight of birds or the entrails of snakes,' she said. 'I see them in my dreams. All I need is a bed to sleep in.'

'And that you shall have,' confirmed Valens. He summoned a female slave from his retinue. 'Take this girl back to the house,' he told her, 'and give her a bath, some clean clothing and something to eat.' He turned back to Atia. 'I look forward to continuing this conversation later.'

Atia gave a solemn bow, almost as if this was nothing less than she had expected. She left with the attendant.

Valens caught sight of Lucius's stare and murmured to him: 'I've been having restless nights lately. Bad dreams. I'm sure that fate has brought this girl to me.'

A horn sounded from below, heralding the start of the afternoon's spectacle: the gladiators! In the seats below and to the right of the podium, some late arrivals were taking their seats. With a shock, Lucius saw that among them was his uncle Ravilla. Valens, always alert to the moods of those around him, saw Lucius flinch.

'What is it?' he asked.

'Nothing,' said Lucius, looking straight ahead and turning his face into a mask.

Valens surveyed the section of the crowd where Lucius had been looking, but luckily didn't seem to recognise Ravilla.

The first contest was between a pair of Equites – mounted gladiators. They trotted into the arena on fine white horses and did several circuits, accepting the applause of the crowd, as the master of ceremonies introduced them and listed their victories. They wore colourful cloaks, metal armguards on their sword arms and brimmed helmets adorned with two feathers. After stationing themselves at opposite ends of the arena, they spurred their horses and charged at each other with lances raised. The crowd cheered as they clashed in the centre, each with his small round leather shield successfully deflecting the other's lance.

Both quickly wheeled their horses and returned to the attack. The red-cloaked Eques was fractionally quicker in the turn than his blue-cloaked opponent, and charged him down. Blue Cloak managed to raise his shield just in time to deflect another fierce lance blow, but could not prevent himself toppling from his horse. Red Cloak quickly dismounted, unsheathing his gladius. Still on the ground, Blue Cloak used his shield to fend off Red Cloak's stabbing thrusts before rising to his feet, drawing his gladius and resuming battle on more equal terms. After a fierce fight, Blue Cloak was triumphant, driving Red Cloak to the perimeter wall and pressing the tip of his sword to his opponent's throat. The crowd seemed inclined to be merciful, their blood lust apparently sated by the earlier execution. To roars of approval, Valens smilingly raised both his hands, covering his left thumb with his right hand – the sign that Red Cloak's life should be spared.

Next on the programme was the contest between Quin and Vibius Balbo. Lucius's heart beat faster than the drum on a quadrireme* as he watched the small figure of his brother stride into the sunlight. Balbo, the local favourite, swaggered in alongside him. Behind them walked their attendants. Balbo looked about a head taller than Quin, and a good deal broader through the chest and shoulders. Lucius reminded himself that a Retiarius like Quin was traditionally smaller than his opponents – his strengths being agility and fleetness of foot. All the same, Balbo looked like a formidable adversary. He had a shock of thick, dark hair and a scarred yet handsome face, which explained his popularity with the women of Pompeii. But it wasn't his face that Lucius was concerned about – it was his muscles, which rippled beneath his gleaming chest and torso like coiled serpents.

Balbo raised his giant arms, the right one enclosed in a metal guard or manica tied with leather thongs. A great roar went up from the crowd as the local supporters chanted their favourite's name: 'Bal-bo! Bal-bo! Bal-bo!'

With a chill, Lucius sensed a new mood overtaking the audience. They had enjoyed the Equites in a tolerant, restrained spirit befitting a piece of lunchtime

---

* *quadrireme: a warship with four rows of oars. A drum was beaten to help the rowers keep in time.*

entertainment – but now, with the arrival of Balbo, the crowd's inner barbarian had been reawoken, and with it their blood lust. Quin would have to win this duel, because if he lost they would undoubtedly demand his death.

The attendants handed the fighters their weapons and armour. Balbo was given a helmet and a large, rectangular shield. The helmet, when he put it on, completely enclosed his head and fanned out at the base to give protection to his neck and upper shoulders. His face was now completely masked, except for two circular eyeholes. The effect of this crested metal head with black, malevolent eyes surmounting a giant, muscular body was truly intimidating. He looked scarcely human, like a monster from some ancient Greek myth. Lucius was desperately scared for Quin. He secretly rubbed his father's ring, hoping it would bring luck.

His brother was putting on a brave face. He had faced countless Secutores in practice bouts, and had already bested one in the arena. Yet he'd never faced a hostile crowd like this one, and that must surely be affecting him. Still somehow managing to smile confidently, Quin moved towards the middle of the arena and raised his net and trident towards his own contingent of supporters, who had travelled all the way from Rome. They cheered enthusiastically, and Lucius would have joined in if he hadn't been standing on the editor's podium. In any case, the cheers were almost completely drowned out by the thundering chorus of boos from the locals.

Quin wore a manica and a shoulder guard on his left arm, but was otherwise defenceless – no helmet, shield or any other armour. Like Balbo, his only clothing was a loincloth. While Balbo was armed with a gladius, Quin carried a net, a trident and, in his belt, a pugio – a straight-bladed dagger.

A soldier raised a large, curved ram's horn to his lips and gave a loud blast, signalling that the contest should begin. The two fighters began to circle each other. Quin's net dangled from his right hand, its end dragging through the arena dust. In his left hand he carried the trident, its prongs pointing at his opponent, its shaft parallel to the ground. It was vital to keep his distance during the fight. At close quarters, the Secutor always held the advantage.

Lucius could see Quin's eyes fixed on Balbo, sensitive to his smallest movements, assessing his strengths and weaknesses. Balbo looked content to bide his time, barely advancing as the two skirted each other.

Suddenly, Quin danced closer and jabbed at Balbo, forcing the bigger man to parry with his shield. As he raised his gladius to counterattack, Quin retreated. Not long afterwards, Quin lunged again, then drew back. This pattern continued for the next few minutes, with Quin making sudden darting attacks followed by swift withdrawals.

'Your brother fights cleverly,' Valens murmured to Lucius. 'He's trying to exhaust the Secutor by forcing him to keep raising that heavy shield. The longer the fight goes on, the better the chances for the Retiarius.'

Soon after he said this, Quin sprang another attack. This time, when Balbo parried, instead of retreating, Quin threw his net. The circular mesh had tiny weights at its perimeter, so that it fell quickly over Balbo. The move caught the Secutor by surprise. His shield got caught in the net, and he only just managed to disentangle himself before Quin could get close enough to finish him off. The Secutor staggered away to a safe distance. Disappointed, Quin used the drawrope tied to his wrist to return the net to his hand.

The move did at least manage to silence the home supporters. Seeing their champion come so close to a swift defeat was enough to dampen their spirits – albeit briefly. But they were soon roaring their support for Balbo even louder than before. The energy coming from his fans seemed to galvanise Balbo. He squared his enormous shoulders, raised his gladius and charged at Quin with the speed and ferocity of a bull. Quin ducked and parried Balbo's sword blow with the shaft of his trident before thrusting its prongs at the big man's helmeted head. There was a hollow clang, and Balbo stumbled. The trident couldn't pierce the metal, but he'd certainly felt the blow.

Once again, the local champion had been surprised by the challenger's quicker reflexes. But again Quin was slow to take advantage. As he cast his net towards his downed adversary, Balbo hastily rolled out of the way, then grabbed hold of the net before Quin could withdraw it. Seizing it with both hands, the Secutor pulled on it. With his wrist bound to the net, Quin was dragged forward helplessly. Balbo began turning on the spot, forcing Quin to run circles around him. With the crowd egging him on, Balbo turned faster and faster, all the time pulling on his end of the net. Quin was spun around like a discus about to be thrown by an Olympic athlete.

Lucius could only look on in impotent despair as Quin was hauled about – the fisherman caught by his own net. Valens's hand squeezed Lucius's shoulder. 'Don't worry,' he whispered. 'Your brother isn't finished yet.'

Yet Lucius found it hard to draw any other conclusion as he watched Quin lose his footing and fall to his knees. To the guffaws of the delighted crowd, Balbo began dragging the prostrate Quin across the arena, raising clouds of dust as he went. The Secutor laughed and waved to his supporters, adding to their euphoria. They were overjoyed to see the upstart gladiator from Rome humiliated in this way. Even the aediles, Pansa and Sabinus, were giggling.

Balbo was enjoying himself too much to notice Quin draw the pugio from his belt and slice through the rope that bound him to the net. Once free, Quin sprang to his feet and charged at Balbo. The big man turned in surprise and the trident struck him on the manica with an audible crack.

'Yes!' hissed Lucius to himself, and he clenched his fists behind his back in a secret display of triumph.

The jolt caused the Secutor to drop his gladius. As Quin tried to kick it out of the way, Balbo bashed him with his shield, causing Quin to totter, though he managed to stay on his feet. Balbo retrieved his sword and returned to the attack with a series of furious hacking blows aimed at Quin's head. The Retiarius parried these with the shaft of his trident, all the time backing off. With his net gone, it was now a straight fight between gladius and trident, with Quin's dagger held in reserve.

Lucius noticed that Quin wasn't retreating in a straight line, but in a curving path that was gradually bringing him closer to his discarded net. The slashes of Balbo's blade were relentless, and seemed to increase in violence, as if he was getting impatient to close the fight. Lucius gasped as Quin stumbled under an exceptionally hard blow from the Secutor's gladius. The next strike of the blade was so powerful that it broke the shaft of the trident. Quin dropped the useless weapon and tried to flee, but Balbo pushed him over. The Secutor uttered a triumphant roar and plunged the tip of the gladius towards Quin's stomach. Just in time, Quin rolled out of the way, and in the same flowing movement he grabbed his fallen net and flung it at Balbo's legs. The move was so quick, so unexpected, it provoked an audible gasp of shock around the amphitheatre. Perhaps no one in the crowd but Lucius had spotted the net lying there, half obscured in the dust. Quin's throw was good, and the net wrapped itself around the Secutor's feet and ankles. He tried desperately to free himself as his supporters groaned in anguish, but Quin quickly tightened the drawcord, trapping him securely. Then he yanked at the net, making Balbo topple to the ground with a resounding crash. Determined not to miss his opportunity this time, the Retiarius jumped on top of his opponent's chest and pointed the tip of the pugio at his throat.

The home crowd howled their dismay – at least most of them did. But there was also quite a lot of cheering and applause, far more than Quin had mustered on his entry to the arena.

'Your brother's bravery and talent have won him a lot of friends today,' Valens murmured.

Lucius released a long-held, shuddering breath. He let the relief flood through him like a warm river, calming his heart and muscles. Gradually an awareness of his body returned – his hands ached from keeping them squeezed into tight fists, and there was blood on his lip, which he must have been biting without realising.

Balbo raised the index finger of his left hand, asking for mercy. The crowd urged Valens not to let their favourite die, and he duly obliged, offering them the shielded thumb. Quin was awarded a palm branch for his victory, which he waved to the crowd, but he refrained from performing a lap of honour to celebrate his victory, perhaps fearful of the hostility it might provoke. After saluting his supporters, he helped Balbo to his feet, and the two men departed the arena to cheers of acclaim.

CHAPTER V

42 hours before the eruption

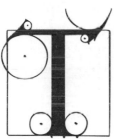

That evening, the animals in the zoo seemed restless. The birds were noisier than ever, and their twitterings were interspersed with regular growls, shrieks, whinnies and trumpetings from the other cages.

Their mood was a topic of lively debate at Valens's party that night, and also provoked an argument in the kitchen. Tirano, the Nubian slave in charge of the animals, came into the kitchen while fresh platters of olives, dates, sardines and eggs were being prepared. He was looking for some fish or vegetables with which to tempt Arto the bear, who was off his food.

'You're not taking any of my lampreys,' said Otho, the head cook, emphatically. 'They were expensively reared in the fish ponds of a friend of the master's at Baiae, and will not be used as fodder for a mangy old bear. Have a few sardines, if you must.'

'What is the matter with those beasts tonight?' asked Gerardus the pastrycook.

Tirano shrugged. 'I've never seen them like this in the ten years I've worked here. The lion, Romaleo, has been throwing himself against the bars, like he's desperate to escape.'

'They know that something is wrong,' said Atia, who was busy peeling the shells from a bowl of hard-boiled eggs. She was now installed in the household as Valens's official augur, but had been temporarily seconded to kitchen duty to help with the catering for the party. The slaves were divided about Atia – as all who met her seemed to be – some she antagonised and others she intrigued.

Mico was one of those whom she intrigued. 'What do they know?' he asked her.

'What do they know? What do they know?' exploded Otho. 'They know nothing. They're stupid animals. Good for nothing but their meat and milk.' He eyed Atia suspiciously. 'The master may have been taken in by you, little one, but that doesn't mean the rest of us are. I suggest you keep your soothsaying mumbo-jumbo to yourself.'

'If you ask me, it's that girl's arrival that's distressing the animals,' commented Fulvia, another kitchen slave. She plucked a live lamprey from a bucket and dropped it into a cauldron of boiling water. Lucius watched the eel-like fish writhe in agony.

Atia continued to peel off eggshells, seemingly unaffected by these remarks. Lucius suspected she was quite used to being treated like an outcast. 'Smell the water,' was all she said.

'Smell the water,' grumbled Otho. 'What does she mean, smell the water? The girl is off her head.'

Fulvia speared the half-boiled lamprey with a long fork and pulled it from the cauldron, then scraped away the first layer of its mottled, greyish-brown skin. With two swift movements of her knife she removed the still-twitching head, and the guts.

'Give me the blood,' instructed Otho, tapping an earthenware pot in front of him. 'The lamprey must be cooked in its own blood.'

Fulvia poured the dark pink translucent liquid into the pot, and Otho added wine, olive oil, vinegar, bay leaf, garlic, pepper and finely chopped cured ham. He began to stir the mixture.

Smell the water.

When no one was looking, Lucius sneaked out into the little courtyard behind the kitchen. A pipe in the wall spouted water into a trough, from where they took it to use for cooking. He cupped some in his hand and sniffed it. There *was* a slight odour to it, and it revolted him. In the kitchen the cooking smells had masked it, but out here it was unmistakable: a smell of rottenness, like bad eggs. *Sulphur!* He wondered what it could mean. Had something contaminated the Aqua Augusta?

'What are you doing out there?' called Otho from the kitchen entrance. 'I need you in here now.'

Lucius approached him. 'You know, Otho – '

'Offer this to the guests,' the head cook interrupted, handing him a freshly prepared platter of canapés. Lucius nodded and took the platter. He decided not to mention the sulphur smell, as that was bound to incense Otho.

As he passed among the guests in the triclinium, Lucius caught sight of Eprius, looking bored as usual. Nearby, his father was sounding off to some local politician on his favourite subject: the ludicrously high taxes levied by the imperial government. Lucius offered Eprius the platter.

Eprius looked up and his face broke into a smile. He took a few olives. 'That was your brother in the arena this afternoon, wasn't it?'

Lucius nodded.

'Now I understand how he was able to fight off those boys the other day.' Eprius's smile seemed paper-thin – a shallow pretence at cheerfulness. The scab on the boy's cheek had faded, but the lines of sorrow were as deeply etched as ever.

'I know about you and Posilla,' whispered Lucius. 'And I'm sorry.'

Eprius blushed and looked down. 'Best not talk about that here,' he said, nodding towards his father.

He managed another quick smile. 'Anyway, it's good to see a friendly face.'

Lucius was about to reply when he caught sight of someone in the corner of the room and his mouth went dry and numb. Standing there, in deep conversation with Cuspius Pansa, was his uncle. Fortunately, Ravilla hadn't spotted him. Nearby stood Valens. He was talking to Eprius's mother, but just happened to be looking in Lucius's direction at that moment. Once again, Valens's sharp eyes missed nothing. He came over and took Lucius aside. 'I saw that same look pass across your face earlier, at the games,' he said softly. 'As if you'd seen a ghost or something. It was your uncle you saw then as well, wasn't it?'

Lucius hesitated for a moment, then nodded.

'Come with me,' said Valens.

Lucius murmured a quick farewell to Eprius, placed the platter on a table and followed Valens to the tablinum next door, then through another doorway into his private inner study. Lucius had never been in here before. A boy was seated at a table, writing with an iron stylus on a wax tablet. He looked up when they came in. Lucius recognised him as one of the youths he'd seen creeping about the place on other occasions. He'd counted at least ten such boys since his arrival here, and none seemed to be part of the household staff – at least they didn't eat with the other slaves, nor share their dormitory.

'Leave us, please, Sextus,' said Valens.

Without a word, the boy got up from the table and departed, taking the tablet and stylus with him.

'Who was he?' Lucius asked, sensing he was now at a stage with Valens where he could ask such questions.

'Oh, just someone who works for me,' answered Valens vaguely.

It occurred to Lucius then that Valens was a lot better at asking questions than answering them. He knew a great deal about Lucius, but Lucius couldn't say he knew much at all about Valens. In fact, he probably knew more about the life of Romulus, the legendary founder of Rome – the subject of a fresco that dominated one wall of the room – than he did about his own master.

'Tell me, Lucius,' said Valens. 'What is the story with your uncle? Why does he give you the shivers every time you set eyes on him?'

Lucius gnawed on his lip, unsure what to say. He would have loved to tell Valens his suspicions about Ravilla, but he was scared of the consequences for himself and his family.

'I'm concerned about you,' said Valens gently. 'I want you to be happy. If Ravilla is causing you problems, then maybe I can help.'

Lucius looked him in the eye. 'Ravilla is my family's protector, now my father has gone. If anything happens to him, my family will be…' He trailed off.

Valens smiled. 'Alone in the world? Destitute? Do you think I would let that happen?' He put his arm protectively around Lucius's shoulder. 'You shouldn't have to live in fear, Lucius,' he said. 'Your father wouldn't want that. If this man is threatening you in some way, you must tell me.'

'Why are you doing this?' asked Lucius, suddenly suspicious. He broke out of Valens's embrace. 'Helping Eprius and Posilla by giving them a place to meet once a week is one thing. But why would you go up against a man like Ravilla – for *my* sake? It doesn't make any sense.'

Valens leaned against the side of the desk and looked down. 'Your father was an inspiration to me, Lucius,' he said quietly. 'He taught me more about the meaning of *virtue* than any philosopher I've ever read, simply by the way he conducted himself. He helped me. You might say he changed my life. I owe your father a great deal, and perhaps this is my way of repaying him.'

It warmed Lucius's heart to hear these words. He felt as though his father was near, still influencing his life, still protecting him, even if he was doing so through another man. It was time to confide in Valens.

'I think it was Ravilla who told the authorities that my father was the Spectre,' he said.

'Really!' said Valens, surprised. 'Why Ravilla?'

'Because he hates my father. I've found curse tablets in his secret office. He called on Charon, the death-bringer, to kill him.'

'So he hates his brother,' said Valens. 'That doesn't prove anything.'

Lucius sat down on the chair by the desk and gathered his thoughts. Ravilla's guilt seemed so obvious to him, but clearly he would have to work a bit harder to convince Valens. He turned to face him. 'You remember I told you on the first day I came here about that gladiator called Rufus, who came to our school in Rome?'

'The one who was secretly working for your father, and was then killed in the arena before he could lead you to him?'

Lucius nodded. 'What I didn't tell you was that Ravilla had fixed Rufus's fight. It was something he did on a regular basis as a money-making scheme – Crassus, the school's lanista, was in on it, too. Ravilla told Rufus to lose, but promised him he'd spare his life.'

'So then why did he order Rufus's death?'

'Because, shortly before the fight, he'd overheard my conversation with Rufus. He knew Rufus was planning to take me to my father after the fight, and he wanted to stop that from happening.'

'He sounds like a man with something to hide,' said Valens thoughtfully. 'And ruthless, too.'

'There's something else,' said Lucius. 'I don't know if this is significant or not, but in a message my father sent to me, he said that proof of his innocence exists, but he needed me to get hold of it for him. Now, why couldn't he send a friend or a slave to fetch it? Why did it have to be me? Maybe because the proof is hidden in the house of a member of the family – in Ravilla's house, perhaps? And only a member of the family can enter it without raising suspicions.'

'You may have a point,' said Valens. He looked pensive. 'Leave this with me, Lucius,' he said after a while. 'I have contacts in Rome. I'll see what I can find out... In the meantime, you'd better return to your duties if you don't want Otho to get as steamed as one of his oysters.'

Valens led the way out of his study and back across the tablinum. 'Oh, Lucius,' he said, before they parted. 'Bring Atia into the triclinium, will you? I'd like to introduce her to my guests.'

'So, it's the disappearing boy,' said Otho as Lucius re-entered the kitchen. 'The one who vanishes in a puff of theatrical smoke whenever there's any work to be done. Where have you been all this time?'

'The master would like his guests to meet Atia,' said Lucius, ignoring the question. 'Do you mind if I take her?'

'Of course not!' cried Otho. 'Take the pint-sized witch by all means. Let her spread her poisonous nonsense somewhere else. If the master and his guests wish to pretend to find wisdom in her gibberish, that is up to them. I'd sooner not have her around here distracting my staff.'

Atia stopped what she was doing, wiped her little hands on a towel and jumped down off her stool. Lucius led her down a corridor and into the triclinium.

As soon as she entered, she attracted stares from the guests. Small though she was, Lucius thought that she had what the Greeks called 'charisma' – a mysterious, god-given grace. It wasn't just her remarkable eyes, but her whole expression, so calm and wise for one so young.

'This is Atia,' said Valens, 'whom I have employed as my augur, to divine and interpret the will of the gods. Does anyone care to put her to the test?' His eye sought out one particular guest, who was at that moment staring with astonishment, not at Atia, but at Lucius. 'Ravilla, how about you?' Valens chuckled. 'Ask her anything you like.'

Ravilla's mouth dropped open, then snapped shut. His eyes darted suspiciously from Lucius to Valens and back again. Then, seeming to recover his poise, he took a step closer to Lucius and said with a thin-lipped smile: 'Well, perhaps she could start by telling me why my nephew is now working for *you*, Valens.'

Everyone in the room laughed, none more loudly than Valens. 'Maybe it was because you sent him to Pompeii for no apparent purpose,' he chortled. 'He was kicking his heels down at the Schola Armatorum, so I took him on here. I do wonder *why* you sent him to Pompeii, Ravilla. Was he being troublesome in Rome?'

Ravilla stopped smiling. He gave Lucius a stare that sent ripples of ice water through the boy's insides. Did he suspect that Lucius had said something to Valens?

'But surely you have a question of more significance,' Valens cajoled him. 'Are you not be interested in what fate might hold in store for you?'

Ravilla cast a contemptuous eye over Atia.

'Or, if the future does not interest you,' persisted Valens, 'how about asking her something about your past?'

Ravilla looked up at him sharply. He appeared almost like an augur himself at that moment, trying to divine meaning from Valens's enigmatic smile.

'I'm not sure I care for these kinds of games,' he murmured.

'Atia,' said Valens, 'tell us what you see.'

Atia reached up and clutched Ravilla's forearm, making him wince. She stared up at him, and his face seemed almost to gleam in the bright intensity of her gaze. The room was now silent, and Lucius was aware of the other guests leaning forward, waiting to hear what the girl would say. Even Crispus seemed to find this sideshow temporarily more fascinating than the sound of his own voice. As for Lucius, he was so tense he could scarcely breathe. Would she reveal, in front of everybody, that Ravilla had made false accusations against his own brother, forcing him into exile? Such a claim, even from a seven-year-old street prophetess, could very easily catch the ear of the gossipmongers in the Forum – first here, and then back in Rome. It could lead to Ravilla's ruin. The thought excited but also terrified Lucius, for he wondered how Ravilla would react. Would he exact violent revenge on Atia, or Valens – or even on Lucius, if he thought him involved in some way?

Right now, Ravilla looked embarrassed and scared as he tried to free his arm from Atia's grip – and that was satisfying for Lucius to see. In his experience, Ravilla was always the one in control of events – the master manipulator. But this double-act of Valens and Atia had wrong-footed him, caught him unawares, and now, in front of the great and good of Pompeii, he looked vulnerable.

'I see you as a boy,' said Atia in a soft, low voice. 'You are with your brother, Aquila, on one of the hills above Rome...'

Hearing this, Ravilla seemed to relax, and a thin smile appeared on his face. Lucius felt disappointed. Was this going to be nothing but a harmless childhood anecdote?

'You are on the Capitoline Hill,' continued Atia, 'walking near the southern summit. Near the Tarpeian Rock...'

The smile fled from Ravilla's face. His lips hardened into a snarl.

'No one is there but you and your brother,' said Atia, her eyes now closed, her face frowning in concentration. 'You dare him to stand at the very edge of the cliff – the cliff where so many murderers and traitors have been forced to stand before being thrown to their deaths on the dagger-sharp rocks below. Your brother accepts the challenge and goes and stands there, at the very edge of the cliff. You are just behind him. You want to push him off. You want to kill him. You think it would be a very fitting death for the brother you have hated all your life. You are already planning how you will explain it to your parents – how the wind blew up suddenly and carried him over. A tragic accident... You creep closer. You reach out to push him... But then, a kestrel screeches. Your brother turns in surprise. You leap backwards. He stares at you, and you laugh. Then he moves away from the summit, and you continue with your walk. Nothing is said. But the question remains, and has burned inside you ever since: did he know what you were planning? Did he know that you wanted to kill him? The answer... The answer...' Her eyes flickered open. 'I... I don't know. I cannot see into his heart.'

Ravilla tore his arm from her grip and staggered backwards. He was gaping at her as if she were some kind of evil spirit, some gorgon from a nightmare. Then, as he gradually became aware of the puzzled stares he was attracting, he straightened his back and tried to regain his composure. Massaging his arm where she had gripped it, he turned to Valens and his fellow guests and uttered a nervous laugh.

'Well,' he said, 'I must say, the girl has quite an imagination!'

There were a few sniggers around the room.

'She had me gripped – in more ways than one,' he chuckled, holding up his arm. 'Where did you find her, Valens? At the theatre? This isn't augury, it's art. I suggest you put her on the stage.'

Valens laughed. 'You may well be right, Ravilla. And thank you for being such a good sport.' He turned to the other guests. 'Now, is anyone ready for another drink? Lucius, if you would be so kind…'

The spectacle was over, and individual conversations resumed around the room. Atia returned to her duties in the kitchen, and Lucius went around refilling goblets. When he reached Ravilla, his hand shook as he poured the wine.

'I don't know what Crassus was thinking of, letting you work here,' Ravilla hissed at him. 'I want you back at the Schola Armatorum first thing tomorrow morning. Clear?'

Lucius's spirits slumped. Not only had Ravilla survived the evening, he had Lucius back under his control – and there was nothing Valens could do about it. Or was there? With a faint surge of hope, Lucius wondered whether Crassus's agreement with Valens carried any legal weight: perhaps Valens would be able to prevent Ravilla from taking him back – at least temporarily.

'But Valens – ' he began.

'Don't you worry about Valens,' snarled Ravilla. 'I'll deal with him.' He looked over to where Valens was standing. 'I'm going to have a private conversation with that man as soon as I can get him away from his guests.'

A short while later, Lucius returned to the kitchen and began helping to prepare the dessert platters: grapes, figs, peaches, cherries, apricots and plums all had to be washed, chopped and have their seeds or stones removed. Walnuts, hazelnuts, almonds and chestnuts had be shelled. As he worked, his mind was still buzzing with the scene he'd just witnessed. Ravilla had actually looked scared as Atia held him in her grip. Lucius glanced at her, perched on her stool on the far side of the table. As she peeled a pomegranate and removed its pulpy pink seeds, she looked so innocent, so like an ordinary little girl. How amazing it was that this child, who this morning was living in the gutters of Pompeii, could have held, for just a moment, the power to destroy one of the cleverest operators in Rome – yet now appeared utterly unaffected.

When Lucius returned to the triclinium, Valens and Ravilla were nowhere to be seen. Perhaps Ravilla had persuaded his host to have that 'private conversation'. Lucius would have given anything to be able to listen in. He circulated among the guests, offering them fruit from the platter.

A touch on his arm made him turn. It was Eprius, looking flustered and a little breathless, as if he'd just come running in from somewhere.

'Fruit?' asked Lucius with a smile. 'Or would you prefer to wait for Otho's famous honey-soaked cake?'

Eprius shook his head. 'Can you get away for a few minutes?' he whispered urgently. 'There's something I think you should hear.'

Lucius frowned, puzzled and intrigued. He glanced around. 'No Otho in sight,' he whispered. 'And the master's otherwise engaged. I should be OK for a bit.'

He put down the platter and followed Eprius into the tablinum, from where they turned left through an arched doorway into the darkness of the peristyle. The night air was hot and heavy, the sweet scent of the herb garden tinged with a faint stench of animal dung. The zoo, at least, seemed calmer now.

'Where are we going?' Lucius asked as they turned right and began walking along the columned porch bordering the garden.

Eprius hushed him by putting a finger to his lips. 'Your uncle is meeting with Valens,' he said.

'I know,' said Lucius sadly. 'He wants to tell him that he's taking me back to the Schola Armatorum – but I'd much rather stay here.'

'Then maybe your uncle doesn't know Valens very well,' said Eprius.

Lucius brightened. 'You mean Valens will insist on keeping me?'

'I don't know,' said Eprius. 'Maybe. But I don't think the conversation is going to be about that. I was listening to the start of it, and – '

'Wait a minute,' Lucius interrupted. 'What do you mean, you were listening? How?'

'That's what I brought you here for,' whispered Eprius, beckoning him further along the peristyle. He stopped a few paces short of the corner, knelt down and began very stealthily removing a loose sandstone brick from the villa wall. Lucius calculated that they had progressed beyond the end of the tablinum and were now alongside Valens's private study. Was Eprius really offering him a way of eavesdropping on the conversation?

'I've spent a lot of time at this house over the past few months,' Eprius whispered as he worked at the brick, sliding it out bit by bit. 'I discovered this loose brick a few weeks ago. I worked out that on the other side of this wall is the room where Valens conducts all his private business. Every day I gradually worked it looser until…' The brick finally came free, and he gently placed it on the flagstone floor. 'Now have a listen.' He indicated the pitch-black rectangular space he'd created in the wall.

Lucius knelt down and put his ear to the hole. At first he couldn't hear anything. Then someone spoke. It was Valens, his voice sounding strangely harder than normal.

'I know all about you, Ravilla,' he said. 'I know who you are, and why you accused your brother of being the Spectre.'

Lucius's mind was sent reeling by this. He'd never guessed that Valens was going to be so direct and aggressive.

'I?' came Ravilla's nervous laugh. 'Accuse my own brother?' His voice sounded scarily loud and close, as if he were only a hand's breadth away. Lucius leapt back in fright.

'It's OK,' whispered Eprius. 'There's a cabinet standing in front of this hole. They can't see us.'

Nervously, Lucius again put his ear to the hole. His fascination with the confrontation between Valens and Ravilla transcended – for now, at least – his fear of getting caught.

'I think you must have been influenced by that little augur of yours,' Ravilla continued. 'The truth is, I love my brother and would do anything for him. In fact it was I who helped him escape from Rome. I've spent a small fortune getting him away safely and now looking after his family. Speaking of which, I must insist you release young Lucius – '

'Liar!' said Valens, cutting off Ravilla's smooth flow with a harsh shout. 'You didn't *help* your brother flee, you *forced* him into it. You informed against Aquila, as you have informed against so many in your long career – '

'What did you say?' demanded Ravilla, now sounding very alarmed. 'What in Jove's* name are you talking about?'

'You know exactly what I'm talking about, Ravilla. Or should I call you… Spectre?'

---

* *Jove: another name for Jupiter, the father of the gods.*

CHAPTER VI

22 AUGUST

39 hours before the eruption

 ilence followed – a silence so deep and intense that Lucius was starting to worry that Valens and Ravilla could hear his own breathing, which sounded loud and agitated in his ears. Had he imagined it, or had Valens just accused Ravilla of being the Spectre? He looked up at Eprius. The voices must have been clear enough for him to hear as well, because the boy stared back at him, looking as shaken as Lucius felt.

Could Valens be right? It would make a lot of sense, based on what Lucius knew of Ravilla's character and actions. But if it *was* true, how could Valens possibly know about it? He barely knew the man, and had only this evening learned of Lucius's suspicions about him.

There seemed to be only one possible explanation for Valens's words: he was bluffing!

'It's time I departed,' said Ravilla, his voice thick with suppressed anger. 'Please have your steward fetch my litter.'*

'This conversation is not over!' barked Valens.

'I'm afraid it is,' said Ravilla. His voice was more muffled now, and Lucius guessed he must have moved to the study door. 'Your words and actions tonight have told me all I need to know about the kind of man you are, Marcus Nemonius Valens. First you steal my nephew. Then you try to humiliate me in front of your guests by staging that absurd bit of theatre with the street child. And now you start flinging ridiculous and slanderous allegations at me. I don't believe we have anything more to say to each other.'

'Very well, then,' responded Valens. 'Leave if you must. But be aware that I can back up this allegation. If you step out of that door now, I will go straight to the praetor in Rome and present him with incontrovertible proof that you are the Spectre.'

Lucius's jaw dropped open when he heard this. *Proof!* What possible proof could Valens possess?

'This is preposterous,' he heard Ravilla mutter, and from the broken quality of his voice he sounded as stunned as Lucius himself. 'You don't know me. I don't believe we've ever even met before tonight.

* *litter: a chair or bed carried on poles.*

How can you possibly have proof of something that isn't even true?'

'Come now, Ravilla,' chuckled Valens. 'There's no need to play the innocent with me. You know as well as I do that a written document exists that proves you are the Spectre, and you also know what that document is. Do you want me to spell it out for you? Perhaps I should call in that gossipmonger Cuspius Pansa from next door and spell it out to him, too? Would you like me to do that?'

'This is all a bluff,' sneered Ravilla. 'You don't have proof of anything.'

'Do you really want to take that risk?' Valens challenged him. 'Imagine the consequences if you're wrong. Aquila returned from exile, acquitted and restored to his family. You, humiliated in front of your senatorial peers. Stripped of your land, rank and possessions. Forced to live out the rest of your days in miserable exile. You're not like your brother, Ravilla. He has his books to sustain him. You wouldn't survive a month in that kind of isolation.'

There followed another long silence, and the atmosphere seemed to grow even hotter and denser. Lucius noticed that his tunic was damp with sweat. Eprius was crouching in the shadows close by, listening intently.

Eventually Ravilla responded, in a voice that seemed to emerge from a deep well or from a sepulchre. 'You have the letter, then?'

Hearing this, Lucius clamped a hand over his mouth to prevent himself from gasping.

Valens must have nodded, for Ravilla went on: 'The letter from the last emperor, from Vespasian, confirming that I am the Spectre?'

'Indeed I have,' said Valens, speaking more gently now, more like the Valens that Lucius knew.

There was a sharp bang, as if a piece of furniture had been struck hard by a hand. 'I knew that a copy of that letter must exist somewhere!' said Ravilla, sounding furious. 'But how did you, of all people, get hold of it? You're nothing but the son of a freedman,* living in a provincial backwater. A zookeeper, for Jove's sake!'

'I'm better connected than you might imagine,' said Valens, seemingly unaffected by Ravilla's attempt to insult him. 'But let's not concern ourselves with how I got the letter. Let's talk instead about what we're going to do about it.'

Lucius was filled with awe at the artful game Valens had just played. Using nothing more than inspired guesswork and shameless bluffing, he had managed to persuade Ravilla to confess to being the Spectre. How had he known? When had he guessed? Was it when Atia told that story? Lucius didn't even care. All that mattered was that Valens had done it – he'd exposed Ravilla! And now he was going to force him to confess his crimes to the highest authorities in Rome. And

* *freedman: an ex-slave who has been set free by his master or mistress as a reward for good service.*

then Lucius's father could return, his name cleared of all wrongdoing. Lucius grinned jubilantly at Eprius, and was surprised when the boy didn't smile back.

Then Valens spoke again: 'I don't want to see you fall, Ravilla. If we can reach a satisfactory agreement, that letter need never see the light of day.'

Lucius nearly choked when he heard this. Eprius appeared to be blinking back tears.

'You're... you're talking about blackmail!' cried Ravilla.

'Such an ugly word,' said Valens mildly. 'Think of it more as a business arrangement. You've done something wrong. Sooner or later someone was bound to have discovered the truth. Count yourself lucky it was me. I'm offering to keep it a secret between us – and I mean between *us*. Believe me, I will police this secret as vigilantly as if it were my own reputation on the line. If I discover anyone threatening to expose you, I'll deal with them ruthlessly. In return for this protection, all I ask from you is the payment of a simple monthly fee of fifty denarii.'*

Hearing this, Ravilla uttered an inarticulate cry of rage. 'Robber!' he bellowed when he could speak again. 'How dare you?'

'Why is Valens doing this?' Lucius mouthed to Eprius.

'This is what he does,' Eprius whispered back.

---

* *fifty denarii: it would take an ordinary soldier or labourer about seven weeks to earn this amount.*

'Fifty denarii!' wailed Ravilla. 'I told you earlier how financially stretched I am, having to keep my accursed brother's family – not to mention the expense of running a gladiator school.'

Valens laughed at this. 'Yes, well I'm sure that particular expense is more than offset by your habit of fixing gladiator fights and then betting on the outcome!'

Ravilla groaned.

'Let's not be modest about your wealth, Ravilla,' continued Valens. 'I've no doubt you've got your finger in lots of pies, not all of them entirely savoury. I could, of course, widen my offer of protection to embrace your entire portfolio of illegal activities, and charge you a good deal more for the privilege, but I don't want to be greedy. Fifty denarii is my price, payable monthly in advance, and in return I offer you complete peace of mind.'

'You scoundrel!' muttered Ravilla.

Lucius's head was spinning. Was this some sort of elaborate game Valens was playing? Surely he wasn't really going to blackmail Ravilla?

Lucius was getting cramp in his legs from crouching for so long. He shifted his position to get more comfortable and, in doing so, he nudged the brick by his knee, making a loud scraping sound on the flagstones.

'What was that?' asked Ravilla in alarm. 'Is someone listening to us?'

Lucius froze, staring fearfully at Eprius.

'It sounded as though it came from behind that cabinet,' he heard Valens say.

There was a rumble of furniture being moved. Eprius quickly replaced the brick; a glimmer of lamplight appeared in the hole just as he slid the brick home. They waited, as still as statues, scarcely daring to breathe. The sweat tickled as it dripped down Lucius's forehead and nose, but he dared not wipe it away. Then they heard running footsteps in the tablinum. Lucius was too scared to move.

'Quick!' hissed Eprius, pulling him to his feet and yanking him further along the peristyle. They skidded round the corner and dashed down the long covered border of the rectangular garden, past the exedra, where only the day before Valens had explained to Lucius how he wished to use his wealth to help others. Out of the corner of his eye, Lucius glimpsed torchlight behind him, at the archway that led into the tablinum. He heard footsteps again, slower this time. He pictured the two men stopping to examine the wall next to Valens's study. They would almost certainly find the loose brick.

Lucius followed Eprius into the lobby, then through a doorway on the right, next to the one that led to the bath-house. They found themselves in a long, narrow room – almost a corridor. In the gloom, Lucius glimpsed bare brick walls with a shelf along one side containing wooden-soled sandals, jugs of olive oil and strigil blades. Eprius tugged his arm and led him to the end of the room, then down a small set of curving steps. The air below ground level was hot and dry. In the light of the glowing embers of a furnace, Lucius saw they were in a cramped basement area with soot-blackened walls.

'This is the fire that heats the hypocaust* for the bath-house,' said Eprius, crouching to avoid hitting his head on the low ceiling. 'I think the slave in charge of the furnace has gone to bed now. We should be safe here – for a while.'

They sat down on the floor. Lucius looked at Eprius's troubled face, shining in the glow of the flickering embers. 'Tell me this is all part of Valens's bluff,' Lucius said. 'He's not really going to blackmail my uncle, is he?'

Eprius nodded sadly. 'I'm afraid so,' he said. 'Valens isn't the man you think he is.'

'But he's helped *you*, hasn't he?' Lucius pointed out. 'He's offered you and Posilla a place to meet each week.'

Eprius gave a choked sort of laugh. 'Yes, that's how Valens always likes to describe his "services" – as if he's doing everyone a favour! I don't suppose he mentioned that the services he offers aren't free.'

'You mean you have to *pay* him?'

'Of course! Ten denarii a month!' Eprius gave another short, hollow laugh. 'And I can't even afford it!'

---

* *hypocaust: a system of underfloor heating. The floor is raised on short brick pillars and hot air from a furnace circulates between them.*

'Why ever did you agree to the deal?'

Eprius looked at Lucius as if shocked by his innocence. 'Do you think I had any choice? Valens found out about me and Posilla. Then he had a conversation with me, just like the one he had with your uncle just now. He said I was lucky that he was the one who'd discovered us. He said he'd offer us his protection, and a place to meet each week, in return for a monthly fee. When I refused, he threatened to tell my parents. That was six months ago. Posilla and I are completely in his power, and now your uncle is, too. This is what Valens does. It's how he makes his money, and it's why he's so influential in Pompeii. He knows everyone's dark secrets, including all those aediles and duovirs and the other city bigwigs who come to his parties. If he wants them to decide a court case in his favour, they'll do it. If he wants an extra water pipe diverted from the aqueduct to his property, they'll give it to him. He seems nice enough on the surface, but everyone's terrified of him.'

Lucius stared at the fire. He was struggling to match up the Valens that Eprius was describing with the one he knew. Then he remembered the harsh voice Valens had used when talking to Ravilla, so unlike his usual polite, good-natured tone, and he realised that Eprius must be telling the truth. There were two faces to Valens: the one he wore in public, and the private one he used to terrify his 'customers'. Lucius had just been introduced to the private face.

'But how does he *discover* people's secrets?' he asked Eprius.

'He has a network of boys who hang around the city, loitering in the squares and by the fountains, listening to gossip.'

Lucius recalled all the mysterious youths drifting around the house – it was all starting to make sense.

'They bring him information about gamblers, unfaithful husbands, corrupt judges and politicians,' said Eprius. 'It seems that almost everyone has something to hide in this city, and sooner or later Valens will find them out.'

'I saw a boy here once,' said Lucius. 'He looked like one of those bullies who beat you up. Were they Valens's boys?'

Eprius touched the mark on his cheek and nodded. 'I was late with my payment last month. For all his threats, Valens doesn't actually like revealing our secrets, because once he has, he's got no more hold over us. So he deals with late payers by sending his boys round. It usually does the trick. I managed to find the money – but it's getting harder each month.'

A scary thought suddenly occurred to Lucius. 'What if Valens thinks it was us listening in to his conversation with Ravilla?'

'Then he'd kill us for sure,' replied Eprius in a resigned tone.

Lucius felt sick with fear. He wondered how Eprius could live, day after day, with this threat hanging over him. The boy seemed sad rather than frightened, as if he'd already surrendered to his fate.

'I have to get away from here,' said Lucius.

'If you leave, you'll only make yourself look guilty,' said Eprius. 'Your best hope is to stay put, pretend everything's normal.'

'It's all right,' said Lucius. 'Valens knows that Ravilla wants me back at the Schola Armatorum. He won't suspect a thing.'

The Schola Armatorum didn't exactly feel like a sanctuary now that Ravilla was in residence – but then, after what he'd witnessed tonight, Ravilla seemed like a weak, pale imitation of wickedness compared to Valens.

'What about you?' Lucius asked Eprius.

'I'll be OK,' replied the other boy, '– at least until the next payment is due.' He rose to his feet. 'We'd better get going. Occasionally my father stops lecturing the people around him, and when he does, he might just spot that I'm no longer there.'

The two boys sneaked quietly out of the cellar room, brushed the soot from their clothes and returned to the main part of the house.

PART TWO

THE END OF DAYS

CHAPTER VII

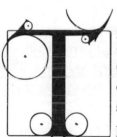he following morning, Lucius awoke early. He got dressed by the grey light of dawn that streamed through the slats of the shuttered windows. After packing his bag, he tiptoed from the dormitory. He left a message for Valens on a wax tablet in the tablinum, apologising for leaving unexpectedly and explaining that he had been urgently summoned to rejoin his familia at the Schola Armatorum. The vestibule was empty – fortunately. He didn't care to try and explain to Marcipor, the porter, why he was going out at such an early hour.

Once outside the house, Lucius broke into a run. The further he went, the more distance he put between himself and Valens's house, the more he began to relax. Even at this hour, the sun already felt warm on his skin. A gentle sea breeze swept through the streets, rustling the leaves. It carried a faint rotten smell from the fish sauce factories around the harbour.

Today was Vulcanalia, the festival to honour Vulcan, the god of fire. In the centre of the Forum, slaves were piling bundles of wood onto a big bonfire for the evening sacrifice. The colonnade was decorated with hanging festoons. Already the city was echoing to the cries of street traders and the drumming of the buskers. Running through the alleys, Lucius narrowly missed being splashed by the contents of a waste bucket poured from an upstairs window.

At first his only desire had been to get away from Valens. Now, as he moved through the crowds along the main thoroughfare heading east, he began to ponder what his next move should be. Ravilla was the Spectre, and that fact had to be revealed to the world somehow, so that Lucius's father could clear his name. He had heard his uncle confess to this, yet he had no proof, and who would believe the word of a servant boy? What was more, revealing this knowledge would put his own life in danger. Valens had sworn that if anyone threatened to expose Ravilla's secret, he would 'deal with them ruthlessly' – which had to mean 'kill them'. Valens would certainly have found the loose brick by now and would be on the lookout for any potential eavesdroppers. Lucius wondered whether he really *was* safe. Otho would tell Valens that he had been missing from the kitchen during the time of the conversation, and Valens's guests could confirm that he wasn't in the triclinium either. Some guests might even have seen him go into the tablinum with Eprius. If Valens did decide that Lucius was the eavesdropper, he wouldn't be safe, even out here in the streets – he would never forget how the bully boys had ambushed Eprius in the alley that day. But the blackmailer might find it harder to extend his lethal power within the walls of the Schola Armatorum – at least Lucius hoped so! As for Eprius – if suspicion fell on him, there probably wasn't much hope for the boy: he was already completely in Valens's power, and Lucius didn't sense that Eprius had much fight left in him.

By the time Lucius reached the frescoed walls of the Schola Armatorum, the city dust was clinging to his sweaty face and tunic, and a plan had formed in his mind. He knocked on the door. It was answered after a long wait by a sleepy young slave named Florus.

'What do you want at this hour?' he yawned. 'Don't you know it's a holiday?'

Lucius gave him his name. 'I work for Crassus,' he explained. 'I'm the brother of Quintus, the Retiarius. You have to let me in.'

Florus opened the door wider, and Lucius slipped past him. He hurried down the passageway that ran the length of the building, past doors leading to the training arena, the weapons room, the trophy room and the dining room, until he came to the dormitory occupied by Quin and his fellow gladiators. He'd decided to take a chance and tell Quin his story. True, his brother got angry whenever their father was mentioned, and believed wholeheartedly in their uncle, but even *he* might be willing to believe that Lucius was on to something, now that Valens had entered the story. Lucius's only hope, he realised, was to tell as many people as he could about what Valens was up to. By spreading the story among many, he would reduce the personal risk to himself and Eprius, and hopefully start a rumour that Ravilla was the Spectre. Quin knew more people than Lucius did, and his word carried greater authority – at least within the familia – so he was the obvious person to start with.

Muffled snores were all that could be heard in the dim dormitory. The air was heavy with slumber. Bodies lay sprawled in various postures, their faces obscured, and it took Lucius a few moments to recognise his brother. He tiptoed over and shook his shoulder.

Quin blinked and gave a start of surprise. 'Lucius? What are you doing here?'

'Get up,' Lucius whispered. 'I have to tell you something.'

'What is it?' Quin didn't look happy at being woken, or at being ordered about.

'I can't tell you here. Meet me in the recreation room as soon as you can.'

Lucius left, hoping that Quin wouldn't just go back to sleep. He passed the time in the recreation room rolling a die on the surface of a wooden table. From the number of sixes he rolled, he quickly reached the conclusion that the die was loaded. Corruption in Pompeii clearly wasn't just a characteristic of the rich and powerful!

He heard a noise in the corridor, like the scrape of a sandal sole, and looked up, expecting Quin to appear. When he didn't, Lucius rose and went to the door. The corridor was empty. A small shiver ran through him, but he told himself to be sensible. It was probably just some early riser making his way to the latrine. Shrugging, Lucius returned to his seat.

A few minutes later, a bleary-looking Quin entered the room. 'This had better be important,' he growled. 'It's supposed to be my day off!'

Beneath the hem of Quin's tunic Lucius noticed deep red scratches on his legs where he had been dragged around the arena by Balbo the previous afternoon. He felt a sudden wave of pride for his brother, the celebrity gladiator, who had won the respect of so many in the home crowd for his courage and skill.

'Congratulations for yesterday,' he said shyly.

Quin nodded and mumbled his thanks.

'I need to tell you something very important,' said Lucius quickly. 'It involves Ravilla and Father, as well as Valens, the man I've been working for here in Pompeii.'

Lucius saw the look of irritation cross Quin's face. 'I don't recognise Aquila as my father any more and

I don't want to hear any more about him,' said Quin. 'Nor do I care to hear any more of your paranoid fantasies about our uncle.'

'I know, I know,' said Lucius, putting up his hands in a placating gesture. 'The thing is, this is bigger than those two now. A very dangerous man has entered the picture. Valens, the man I was working for, is blackmailing Ravilla.'

Quin stared at him. 'Blackmailing? How?'

'He's found out that Ravilla is the Spectre.'

The stare continued for a moment, then Quin's face creased into a derisive laugh. 'Ravilla? The Spectre? Now I've heard everything! Is this really what you dragged me out of bed to tell me?'

'Ravilla confessed to it,' Lucius quickly added.

'Rubbish!' snarled Quin. 'This is another of your delusions, little brother. You probably dreamt it.'

'He didn't dream it,' said a deep voice from the corridor.

They both turned in surprise. From the shadows emerged the short, stocky figure of Crassus.

'Welcome back, Lucius,' said the lanista, examining him with his cold eyes.

At breakfast, Crassus, Lucius and Quin sat together at one end of the long table. Ravilla was nowhere to be seen, so they felt able to talk. Crassus spoke softly and, with all the din coming from the other diners in the room, Lucius had to strain to catch his words.

'I don't believe Ravilla is the Spectre,' said Crassus. 'But I can well believe that Valens tried to blackmail him, considering what happened to me last night. One of Valens's boys was round here, while Ravilla was still at the party at his house. The boy couldn't have been more than sixteen, but very menacing he was. Claimed to know all about the fact that me and your uncle sometimes like to fix the odd gladiator bout. It's trivial stuff, really, but a bit awkward, you know, if it ever got out. Can't think who might have tipped him off.' (He gave Lucius a hard stare as he said this. Lucius looked down, hoping the guilt wouldn't show in his face – he hadn't meant to get Crassus into trouble over the match-fixing.) 'Anyway, I offered the boy a small cut of the profits, as is the usual custom in these situations – but he turned his nose up at that. Said his master didn't like to sully his hands with corrupt practices. That made me laugh. "He's one to talk," I said to the lad, but he didn't even crack a smile. Instead he made his demand: a monthly fee of fifteen denarii. Protection money, he called it. Said that as long as the money was paid each month, me and Ravilla could carry on fixing matches to our heart's content and never need worry about being found out.'

Quin slammed his hand down angrily, making knives and plates clatter all along the table. A few gladiators and servants looked up curiously, but Crassus gave them his chilliest stare, and they quickly turned their eyes back to their plates.

'That man is a leech! A parasite!' said Quin through gritted teeth. 'That's probably how he made enough money to fund these games in the first place! Don't tell me you're going to pay him!'

Lucius stared at his brother, surprised by the ferocity of his reaction. Then he remembered that Valens was attacking the two men on whom Quin's future as a gladiator depended: Ravilla and Crassus.

Crassus shrugged. 'Can't see as I've got much choice.'

'I'm going to say something!' said Quin. 'Let me fight again this afternoon, Crassus, please! The crowd will love it after seeing me yesterday. I'll stand up after the fight, victory palm in hand, and I'll tell them a few home truths about the sponsor of their games.'

'You're doing nothing of the sort!' thundered Crassus. 'We're not here to stir up trouble among the locals. We're here to fight in the games. Understood? And when the games are done, we leave – simple as that. This situation between me and Valens is my business, and it's for me to deal with. I don't want the likes of you poking your nose in. You'll only make things worse. Besides, you're not fighting today. You've had your moment of glory. I'm giving some of the other boys a turn.'

With that, Crassus stood up and stomped out of the room.

'Have you finished with your plate?' enquired a slave who had been hovering nearby.

'What?' Quin glanced at him distractedly. 'Oh, yes. Take it away.' To Lucius, he grumbled: 'I can't believe Crassus. Did you see that crowd yesterday? Doesn't he recognise a star in the making?'

Lucius watched the slave walk off with the plate. The boy seemed familiar somehow, yet he couldn't remember seeing him in the Schola before.

'Is that slave new?'

Quin flashed Lucius an impatient look. 'How should I know? Do you think I notice things like that?' He rose to his feet. 'I'm going off to do some training.'

'What's the point?' asked Lucius. 'You heard what Crassus said.'

'Maybe, if I work hard enough, I can persuade him to change his mind!'

Lucius spent the next few hours doing odd jobs around the building, under the supervision of Piso, the head slave. He helped clean and oil the weapons in the armoury, refilled the lamps with oil and tallow and fetched water from the well. He was sweeping the corridor when Quin came bursting out of the training arena. His sweaty face was glowing with excitement.

'I'm going to fight this afternoon!' he cried.

Lucius clutched his broom handle hard as he looked up at his brother. For some reason, this news disturbed him. 'How come?' he asked. 'I thought Crassus said it was the turn of other fighters.'

'Yes, but then he got this message. It came just a few minutes ago, directly from the sponsor – that snake

Valens. I guess he likes to bask in other people's glory as much as he likes taking other people's money.

'What did the message say?' asked Lucius.

'It said – now, let me think, what did it say?' Quin's brow furrowed as he tried to recall the exact words. 'It said: *After his great triumph yesterday, the people of Pompeii have requested the reappearance of the Retiarius Quintus Felix.*' Quin laughed. 'That's right, Lucius. They want to see me again! Your big brother's famous! OK, I know it's only Pompeii. But if I get this reaction here, after just one fight, imagine what it could be like back in Rome at the Flavian Amphitheatre! When it's finished, they say it'll be able to seat fifty thousand – that's more than double the number here. Can you imagine all those people chanting my name?'

Lucius tried to be happy for his brother. He forced a smile onto his face, but something was troubling him, and it wasn't the usual fear he felt when Quin was due to fight.

'Crassus has forbidden me to say anything afterwards,' Quin was telling him. 'But I'm going to, Lucius. I've got to tell these Pompeiians about the man who's paying for their games.'

'What will you say?' asked Lucius tremulously.

'I'll tell them that this man profits from other people's secrets. He takes their money in exchange for his silence. I was training with one of the local gladiators this morning. I asked him about Valens and he told me there have been rumours about this guy for years – how he's got this network of boy spies going around the city snooping on people. He's hated and feared in this town, Lucius. If I speak out against him, people will welcome it. They'll be cheering me to the skies!'

'No!' said Lucius suddenly.

Quin blinked in surprise. 'What do you mean, *no*?'

'I mean you mustn't. You don't know this man – how dangerous he is. You mustn't say anything.'

Lucius had hoped to convince Quin that Ravilla was the Spectre. If Quin was going to make any sort of speech this afternoon, he wished it could be about that. But, typically, Quin still refused to believe that Ravilla was anything other than their loving, caring uncle. Instead, he'd got it into his head to publicly condemn Valens, the most powerful man in Pompeii, and he was going to do this in front of the entire town, including the man himself! The thought was absolutely terrifying. What kind of vengeance would Valens wreak on Quin? His brother would be in constant danger. He wouldn't be safe anywhere, not even back in Rome. And all for what? What could such a speech possibly achieve? He might embarrass Valens, but he could never destroy him.

'Let's just survive this week and then head back home,' Lucius pleaded. 'This is Crassus and Ravilla's business. It has nothing to do with us.'

Quin shook his head. 'I can't live like you, brother, peeping out from under your shell, forever calculating the consequences of every action. Becoming a gladiator has taught me a few things about life. When you fight in the arena, you live from second to second, always within a sword-stroke of death. That's how I want to live my life: with honesty, in the open air, looking death squarely in the face. That's the Roman way.'

Lucius turned back to his sweeping. 'Then you'll probably die,' he murmured.

CHAPTER VIII

24 hours before the eruption

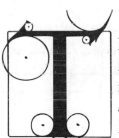

he procession to open the Vulcanalia festivities began at the Forum at midday. Lucius stood in the crowd and watched the parade go by. It was led by a pair of hornblowers and four lictors – bodyguards to the aediles. Behind them walked four slaves carrying a platform on their shoulders. The platform supported a large statue of a blacksmith crouched over an anvil, ready to strike it with a hammer. This was a representation of Vulcan, the god of fire, and – naturally – it was commissioned by the Guild of Blacksmiths, who regarded the festival as a celebration of their profession. A man followed behind, holding up a sign containing the names of Cuspius Pansa and Gnaeus Helvius Sabinus, the aediles co-sponsoring the festival, and Marcus Nemonius Valens, sponsor of the games. Behind this man walked the victorious gladiators of the previous day's games, Quin included, waving their victory palms. As they passed by, they raised the biggest whoops and cheers from the watching crowd. Behind them, slaves carried highly polished samples of gladiator armour and weapons – the finest exhibits of the blacksmiths' craft. Finally, just in front of a trumpeter and a pair of ceremonially attired horses, came the aediles themselves, walking alongside Valens, all of them dressed in immaculate white togas with the purple border worn only by those of high rank.

Lucius shrank back a little as Valens passed, praying he wouldn't be seen. A gentle smile played on Valens's lips as he nodded at the crowds. Then, like a hawk, his darting eyes spotted Lucius. His smile broadened and he came over.

'Lucius!' he beamed, clasping his upper arm like an old friend. 'Isn't this splendid?'

Lucius nodded nervously, finding it hard to look his former master in the eye.

'I'm so sorry you left this morning without even saying farewell,' said Valens. 'I hope all is well with you.'

'Yes, all is well,' blushed Lucius, aware that he was attracting stares from his neighbours.

'I wanted to tell you that I've sent word to Herculaneum to see if anyone there has any knowledge of your father,' Valens continued. 'I'll be sure to let you know if I hear anything.'

'Thank you.'

If Valens did suspect Lucius of listening in on his conversation, he betrayed no sign of it. But this meant little – the man was wearing his public face today.

Lucius cleared his throat. He wanted to say something about Quin and the fact that he didn't think he should fight today, but by the time the words came to him Valens had already said goodbye and returned to his place in the procession.

The crowd followed in the wake of the parade as it made its way slowly east through the city. Most of the shops were closed, their shutters drawn, but the takeaway food counters were doing a roaring trade. People crowded the upstairs windows of the buildings that lined the route, cheering as the procession passed below. Colourful cloths and fabrics were dangling from the window ledges, an ancient tradition at Vulcanalia.

The procession ended at the amphitheatre, but this was merely the start of the day's programme of festivities, which would now continue with an afternoon of gladiatorial games, and then climax with a giant bonfire and animal sacrifices back at the Forum. Outside the amphitheatre, Lucius saw a line of cages and caught a whiff of the animal smell he was familiar with from Valens's zoo. Perhaps today's games would feature a wild beast hunt.

No longer enjoying any special status as an attendant of Valens, he joined the long queues of ordinary citizens waiting to enter the amphitheatre. The queue moved slowly up a long, steep stairway on the outside of the building. From the top of the steps he could look back on a spectacular view right across the city, all the way to the harbour and the glittering haze of the bay beyond. To the north he could see the dark cone of Vesuvius rising above the plain of Campania. Was it an optical illusion or could he see snow near the summit? Snow – on such a hot day? Perhaps it was cloud, though the thin white streaks seemed too solid for that. Then another thought came to him: could it be ash?

The line of people flowed inside the amphitheatre onto a walkway that ran around the top of the seating. The arena looked much smaller from up here than it had from the podium yesterday. The circular clay token, or tessera, that Lucius had been issued with was stamped with an aisle and a row number. He had to walk about a quarter of the amphitheatre's perimeter before he found the appropriate stairway and could make his way down to his place.

A loud trumpet blast signalled the start of the first event. Into the arena charged a snorting, grunting boar, followed by three dogs, a goat and, finally, a large black bear. The boar ran around aimlessly while the dogs chased each other and gnashed their teeth. The goat, which possessed a pair of large, back-curving, fearsomely sharp horns, pawed the ground near the centre of the arena, and the bear loped around the perimeter.

A Bestiarius, or beast fighter, then emerged from the access tunnel of the Porta Triumphalis. His hairless, muscular torso gleamed with oil. He wore padded leather wraps on his arms and legs, and a loincloth. An attendant handed him his galea – a visored helmet with decorative crests – a spear and a whip. Lucius had heard stories of prisoners committing suicide rather than face the wild beasts in the arena. It was hard to imagine anyone volunteering for such a job.

The man strode purposefully towards the bear and cracked his whip under its nose. The bear growled and swung a hairy paw, but the Bestiarius swiftly darted out of its way. Meanwhile, near the middle of the arena, the dogs were circling the goat, snarling and snapping at its hooves. The goat was turning on the spot, seemingly in trouble, but then it suddenly charged, butting one of the dogs in the ribs. The dog let out a whine and scrambled away. The goat turned on the remaining pair of dogs, glowering at them with head bowed, as if daring them to attack. The dogs uttered deep, guttural snarls, but kept their bellies low to the ground, simultaneously threatening and scared.

The Bestiarius was getting the better of the bear, teasing it with the whip and then dodging its attempts to attack. The bear rose up on its hind legs and roared, opening its jaws wide so that every one of its sharp teeth was on display. It swiped and lunged, but the beast fighter was always too quick for it. Meanwhile the boar wandered close to the fight, and the noise and commotion seemed to be upsetting it. Neither man nor bear noticed it lower its head, bare its tusks and paw the ground.

Suddenly, it charged at the man. The spectators screamed their warning, but the Bestiarius didn't seem to hear, or else he misunderstood. Only when the boar was almost upon him did he whirl around and impulsively hurl his spear. The weapon embedded itself in the boar's neck and the creature uttered a very human-like squeal of agony. Its front legs splayed and it fell forward into the dust, its snout only a hand's breadth from its killer's sandals.

While the crowd were still cheering this sight, the bear took a sudden swipe at the fighter's head. There was a horrid crack, heard throughout the amphitheatre, and the man fell unconscious to the ground, his head at an alarming angle to his body. The crowd groaned. Lucius closed his eyes in horror, but too late to avoid the sight of the bear taking a bite from the man's neck, exposing blood, bone and gristle. In less than a heartbeat, this living, breathing man had become a piece of meat. A talented fighter had become a blood-soaked mess, to be hastily removed from the stage. This was how things went at the games, and it only worsened the dreadful foreboding in Lucius's heart. That could so easily have been Quin, he realised. In an hour or so, it could be his brother's corpse they'd be dragging through the Porta Libitinensis.*

Lucius had to get away. His head ached and his stomach felt tight. He couldn't understand how the people around him were able to laugh and eat their bread and sausages. Had they not just seen the death of a man?

He walked hastily towards the exit. As he made his way along the perimeter walkway, he glanced for a final time at the arena and saw the goat, its hind leg in the jaws of one of the dogs, being dragged helplessly backwards. Then he plunged down the long, steep stairs to the plaza outside. He hurried past the street vendors, almost retching at the smell of frying food, until he came to the Palaestra. He had passed this large open space on his previous visit to the amphitheatre. With its lawns, its shady avenues of trees and its swimming pool, surrounded by colonnaded walkways, it seemed like a haven of tranquillity compared to the amphitheatre. Families with young children were picnicking on the lawns or frolicking in the pool.

On a stone bench next to a sundial, he saw a familiar-looking young man with dark curls, sitting by himself. He peered more closely and was delighted to see that it was Eprius. Lucius called his name, and the boy looked up and smiled. He jumped to his feet, and the two embraced like old friends.

---

* Porta Libitinensis: the gateway dedicated to Libitina, goddess of funerals.

'I'm glad to see you're safe,' said Eprius. 'Did you know you were followed this morning?'

'Followed?' gasped Lucius. 'What do you mean?'

'Marcipor, the porter, is a friend of mine,' explained Eprius. 'He lets me know all the comings and goings in that house. He saw you leave early, and then, just a few seconds later, one of Valens's boys slipped out after you. I suppose you went back to the Schola Armatorum, did you?'

'Yes,' croaked Lucius, and he felt a deep shudder inside. He recalled the strange noise he'd heard in the corridor that morning, and the mysterious slave loitering near them during breakfast. So Valens *had* suspected him, and had dispatched a spy. The spy must have overheard everything. Valens must have known, even as he was speaking to Lucius during this afternoon's parade, that Lucius knew what kind of person he really was! The shock of this realisation knocked the breath from Lucius's lungs. He was now in deadly danger – and so was Quin. That message from Valens urging Quin to fight – it wasn't because Quin was popular with the crowds. It was because Quin knew too much about Valens, and now Valens wanted him dead – especially if he knew Quin was planning to speak out against him.

'I have to get back to the amphitheatre!' he cried. 'My brother's in trouble. I have to warn him. This morning I told him everything, and he wants to make a speech after his fight. He wants to tell the crowd about

Valens. But Valens will try and get to him before that, I just know he will!'

'Then come with me,' said Eprius. 'My father and I have seats near the front. Your brother will have a better chance of hearing you from there.'

'But I need to get to him before then – before he enters the arena.'

'It's too late for that,' said Eprius, indicating the sundial. The shadow of the gnomon was pointing to the ninth hour. 'The fight is due to start any minute. We'll have to try and warn him from our seats. Come on!'

As they ran, Eprius tried to reassure Lucius: 'Your brother will probably win the fight, and then Valens can't do anything to him.'

Lucius said nothing. He didn't think Valens was the type to leave such matters to the whims of fate. He probably had some back-up plan in mind to get rid of Quin – assuming Quin wasn't killed before he even stepped into the arena.

At the grand ceremonial entrance on the north side of the amphitheatre, Eprius showed the guards his token and persuaded them that Lucius was a friend and should be admitted with him. Once they were past the guards, they ran up the tunnel, lined with statues and burning torches, and then back out into the daylight. Lucius smelled the perfume-sweetened air and saw that he was surrounded by the clean-shaven, toga-clad Pompeiian elite. He recognised the broad, ruddy features of Bellicianus, sitting with the doughy-faced Priscus in the front row. There were no women in sight, of course – they were seated in another section, much further back from the action. Above and to the left was the podium, where Lucius had stood the day before, attending to Valens. Lucius glimpsed one of the aediles, Cuspius Pansa, sitting there, and just beyond Pansa sat Valens with his chin resting in his hands, looking thoughtful.

Eprius and Lucius took their seats next to Crispus. 'Father,' said Eprius, 'I hope you don't mind – I've invited a friend to join us.'

'Eh? What's that?' said the distracted Crispus. 'No, no, that's fine.' He went back to watching Bellicianus and Priscus, who were sitting a few rows in front of them, right above the perimeter wall. 'How did Bellicianus contrive to get those seats, the wily old snake?' he muttered. 'What are they saying to each other, do you suppose? Of course, they must be talking about me. That slanderous toad! What's he saying? Anyway, I wouldn't take seats in that position even if you paid me. Far too dangerous. I hope Bellicianus gets skewered by a gladiator's spear.'

Eprius and Lucius swapped glances, but Lucius could barely manage a smile, being too eaten up with fear for his brother.

A trumpet sounded below, and into the arena strode Quin. Lucius let out a breath of relief at the sight of his brother looking fit and healthy. At least Valens hadn't managed to get to him *yet*. Quin received a huge cheer from the home crowd. He'd already established himself as a favourite – quite a feat for a gladiator from Rome who'd just beaten the local hero, Balbo. He was followed out by his adversary. The man Quin would have to fight was shorter and broader than Vibius Balbo, and also a lot younger. This lad didn't inspire whistles of adulation from the crowd. He lacked Balbo's good looks and winning smile. In fact, he looked distinctly mean, and there was something about his scowling face that stirred a memory in Lucius.

With a horrid jolt, he realised where he'd seen this person before. He was the young street thug who had very nearly killed Quin on their first day in the city. Lucius saw the same shockwave of recognition strike Eprius. This was one of Valens's boys, hired to beat up Eprius for late payment. And now Valens must have hired the same ruffian to kill Quin, to prevent him revealing Valens's secrets to the crowd. But how could Valens be sure that his boy would be successful? He'd seen how well Quin fought yesterday.

Quin's adversary was introduced to the crowd by the master of ceremonies as Mettius Crito. He was a graduate of the Neronian gladiator school at Capua, founded by the emperor Nero – so he wasn't a local, as Lucius had assumed. Despite his youth, Crito had already won three victories in the arena.

The gladiators' attendants handed them their weapons and armour. Crito was a Murmillo: his helmet had a high red horsehair crest like a fish's fin, a broad rim protecting the face and neck, and an ornate grille-like visor for his face. He wore a loincloth and a belt, a manica on his right arm and a gaiter on his left leg, and he carried a curved rectangular shield. Into his hand the attendant placed a gladius.

Eprius saw it before Lucius. 'The gladius!' he whispered to him.

'What about it?'

'Look at the blade.'

Lucius strained his eyes to see what Eprius was referring to. The blade glinted in the sunlight, and he noticed it was stained purplish-red near the tip.

'What is it? Blood?'

'I fear it may be poison,' breathed Eprius. 'It's the colour of the juice of that berry, belladonna.'

Cool fingers of terror crept across Lucius's skin. 'What's that?' he stammered in a faint, strangled voice.

'Deadly nightshade,' came Eprius's reply. 'Soldiers sometimes dip their swords in it before battle. It's very powerful. I'm afraid he only has to graze your brother with that sword and it will kill him.'

Lucius stood up on shaking legs just as the horn sounded to announce the start of combat. 'Stop the fight!' he screamed, but his voice was lost among thousands as the crowd started to roar. He craned his neck towards the podium. A boy was whispering something in Valens's ear to which Valens was nodding solemnly.

'Stop!' yelled Lucius at the top of his voice. 'Murder!' But he might as well have been whispering in the wind.

CHAPTER IX

21 hours before the eruption

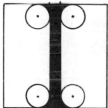n the arena, Quin was doing a good job of keeping clear of Crito's sword. Perhaps he, too, had seen the dark red tip and had worked out what it was. But Crito was beginning to look like a tougher challenge than Balbo. As soon as the horn had sounded, he had come at Quin with a series of powerful lunges. Quin managed to block these with his trident and then swipe at him with his net. But Crito always pulled back too swiftly for him. A stalemate seemed to be developing, with neither fighter able to gain an advantage. This was better news for the lightly armoured Quin, since Crito, with his heavy helmet and shield, was more likely to tire first. Yet, as Lucius was all too aware, Crito only had to scratch Quin with the

tip of his poisoned sword and the fight would be over. It seemed to Lucius that with every clash of sword and trident, Crito was getting closer to his mark. How long could Quin continue parrying before Crito managed to nick his flesh? Lucius prayed for Crito to tire, but the heavily muscled fighter showed no sign of it. His torso was glowing with sweat, but his movements remained just as energetic, just as violent.

Then, from out of nowhere, Quin made a dramatic move – a move he must have practised many times in training, for it appeared so smooth and quick that even the sharp-eyed Lucius failed to see exactly what happened. Crito made his usual lunge, and Quin parried with his trident, then brought his net over his right shoulder as if to whisk it to the left – exactly as he had done the previous dozen or so times. Crito darted to his right to stay clear of the net, but as he did so, Quin suddenly flicked the net leftwards and then whirled it to the right, aiming straight at Crito's head. Crito's own rightward momentum prevented him from changing course, and the net closed around his helmet. Unlike the smooth helmet of the Secutor, the Murmillo's crested headpiece offered plenty of purchase for the net, and Crito was quickly trapped. He flailed helplessly as Quin began to drag him forward. Quin tried to bring the bigger man down onto his knees by making swift tugs on the net. Crito stumbled but managed to stay on his feet and even tried to use their enforced closeness to his advantage. He swung his gladius with blind violence, hoping to land a blow on his captor. Lucius could barely watch as the blade slashed, just a hair's breadth from Quin's stomach. Quin was so busy trying to evade these strokes that he couldn't concentrate on forcing Crito down. Instead he tried running in the other direction, dragging Crito along in his wake. The Murmillo responded by twisting his body around and then wrenching the helmet from his head. He emerged from the net, helmetless, his red face now a mask of fury and hatred. When he saw Crito's expression, Lucius knew that this fight would not end in a friendly embrace, like the contest between Quin and Balbo – it would end in death.

With a scream of rage, Crito ran full tilt towards Quin, who responded by raising his trident. The points of the trident struck Crito's shield with a loud clang. This would normally have been sufficient to halt the attack, but Crito's charge was so fast and wild that Quin was knocked right over onto his back. Crito immediately sprang on top of him. Quin raised the shaft of his trident just as his opponent's gladius came swinging down towards his chest. The middle of the blade embedded itself in the trident shaft. Crito continued to push downwards with brutal force, while Quin used all his strength to thrust upwards. Crito's teeth were gritted, his face contorted into an expression of murderous loathing. The trident trembled in Quin's hands and seemed about to break, as his muscles quivered with exertion.

Lucius saw with deepening despair that Crito was too strong for his brother. The purple tip of the poisoned blade was now just a hand's breadth from Quin's throat and getting closer each second. Soon, either the shaft or Quin's strength would fail, and then it would all be over.

Lucius had his hand in his mouth, fingers pressing hard on his teeth, his muscles tensed as he silently willed Quin to hold out. The crowd around him – hardened as they were by the countless bloody encounters they'd witnessed in this amphitheatre – were stunned into silence. Perhaps it was Crito's unrelenting ferocity, or Quin's desperate determination not to submit, but the roars of excitement died in their throats as they watched this tableau play itself out.

Into this strange silence came a sudden, cracking, thudding boom, as if a giant door had been forced open in the earth. It shook the entire amphitheatre and rolled and echoed around the hollow arena for several seconds like a drawn-out peal of thunder – only this was much louder than any thunder, and it came out of a clear blue sky. Or rather, it didn't come from the sky at all, but from beneath and all around them. There were terrified groans and screams from the spectators. Someone several rows back, with the rough accent of a farmer, cried: 'It's the giants. The giants have come back! I heard them on the mountain last night!'

Down in the arena, Crito, like everyone else, flinched at the sound. For just a second, the downward pressure of his gladius eased, and Quin used the distraction to throw the Murmillo off him and onto his back. Quick as smoke, Quin rose to his feet and pointed the trident prongs at Crito's throat. By the time the crowd had refocused their attention on the gladiators, they saw that the fight was over. Crito appeared almost hysterical. He yelled and rolled his eyes and strained with his fists at the trident prongs, unable to accept that he had lost.

Lucius was too shaken by these fast-unfolding events to fully absorb what had just happened. Eprius grabbed his shoulder and shouted hoarsely in his ear: 'He's done it! Quintus has won!' Finally, reality penetrated and Lucius began to laugh and yell for joy.

'It seems that Vulcan has spoken!' cried Valens, his voice barely audible above the general clamour. Lucius saw that the editor of the games was wearing his usual genial smile, though he did seem somewhat paler than usual. He was looking with extraordinary intensity at the two men in the arena. At first, Lucius assumed that Valens was staring at Quin, but then he thought that maybe he was trying to make eye contact with Crito, who was still raging and struggling with the trident that was pinning him to the ground.

The crowd chanted for Crito's death. They seemed to hate the gladiator and almost fear him, as if he were personally responsible for the colossal boom that had rocked the stadium.

The gods love Quintus Felix,' Lucius heard someone cry out. 'Woe to the man who would slay him!'

'Crito must be sacrificed!' bellowed another. 'Only his death will assuage Vulcan's anger on this day.'

'Death! Death! Death! Death!' chanted the crowd.

At last Crito became calm and seemed to accept his fate. Lucius saw the gladiator's eyes lock with Valens's, then Valens gave a very slight nod – almost a tremble of the head.

'No!' Lucius choked, as sudden, sickening awareness burned through him like stomach acid.

Everyone cheered as Valens thrust his thumb to the side – the sign of death. But before Quin could carry out the people's will, Crito drove his gladius upwards into Quin's leg.

Quin staggered backwards, staring in disbelief at the blood pouring from his thigh. At that moment, pandemonium broke out across the stadium. A roar of fury swelled up from the crowd as a tide of people from the upper tiers left their seats and began to cascade forward, clambering over the more prosperous spectators near the front, then leaping over the perimeter wall into the arena. They came from all sides, converging on Crito in a flood of outraged humanity. Then they fell upon him, pummelling him, tearing at him, pulling him apart. Somewhere deep in the mêlée, Lucius glimpsed a blood-soaked arm wrapped in a manica, fist still clenched, and that was the last he ever saw of Mettius Crito.

Quin just managed to haul himself to the edge of the arena, where he leaned weakly against the perimeter wall. 'Friends!' Lucius heard him cry. 'Romans!' But whatever else he said was lost in all the noise and confusion.

Lucius edged his way to the nearest aisle, then ran down to the bottom step. He scrambled onto the top of the perimeter wall, took a deep breath and jumped down onto the arena sand. Then he pushed his way through the swarms of people to Quin. He found his brother collapsed on the ground, his face pale and shiny with sweat.

'Brother!' gasped Quin feebly, as Lucius went down on his knees and held him in his arms. 'I wanted to speak to them about... to tell them... to...'

He fainted.

'No!' wept Lucius. 'Don't die on me, Quin! I'm going to get you out of here! I'm going to get you to a doctor!' He began dragging Quin towards the Porta Libitinensis. Quin was heavy, and his foot kept getting stuck in his net. But, just as Lucius began to think he wouldn't be able to make it, he heard voices nearby cry out: 'It's Quintus Felix! Help the wounded hero!' Hands grabbed hold of Quin and hoisted him aloft. Lucius ran along behind as an army of Quin's new supporters bore him towards the exit.

'He needs a doctor *now*!' Lucius cried after them. 'He's been poisoned!'

A quarter of an hour later, Lucius was sitting on a chair at the rear of the medical room, watching the doctor work on Quin's leg. The doctor, Aelius Eumenes, was attached to the gladiator school in Rome. Crassus had insisted on bringing him with them to Pompeii because he didn't trust the local surgeons with his valuable men. Lucius was pleased that Eumenes, who hailed from the Greek city of Pergamum, was in charge of Quin's care. Lucius had assisted the doctor several times in the past, and he knew that Eumenes was fond of Quin and would do his best for him. And yet he wondered bleakly what *could* be done. The poison would be acting on Quin already, working its way through his body.

Crassus was also in the room, pacing the floor anxiously. Lucius had told Crassus and Eumenes about the stain on the gladius blade that had inflicted the wound, and at Crassus's request the commander of the guards had sent a contingent of his men back into the arena to retrieve Crito's gladius so that Eumenes could try to identify the poison.

'If it turns out that my boy's been poisoned, I'll want compensation!' ranted Crassus. 'I'll *demand* compensation!'

Lucius hung his head and looked down at his dusty sandals. He tried to block out Crassus's voice. It angered him that the lanista was only ever concerned with the financial value of his gladiators. He seemed to forget that Quin was also a human being – a brother and a son.

Quin emitted a groan of pain. Lucius leapt up and ran over to the table where he was lying. His brother had regained consciousness and was now grimacing as he stared down at his leg. Eumenes had pulled back a loose flap of his flesh with a large pair of tweezers and was pushing a blood-soaked sponge into the wound. 'I've doused this sponge in turpentine,' said Eumenes. 'It will help clean the wound, but it will sting.'

'How are you feeling, Quin?' Lucius asked.

'I've been better,' growled his brother. His head swayed and he went cross-eyed, then collapsed onto his back. 'Aaaah!' he cried.

'Can we give him something to help with the pain?' asked Lucius.

'Mandrake potion will send him back to sleep,' replied Eumenes. 'I sent a slave to the kitchen to make some up a little while ago. Why don't you go and see if it's ready?'

Lucius went down a corridor to the amphitheatre's little kitchen where the gladiators' meals were prepared. A tall, slender boy was stirring a pot containing a thick green liquid.

'Is that the mandrake potion?' Lucius asked.

The boy nodded. 'Go ahead,' he said. 'I think it's ready.'

Lucius used a ladle to scoop some into a goblet, then returned to the medical room. 'Here,' he said gently to Quin. 'Drink this. It'll make you feel better.'

Quin raised himself onto his elbows and bent his head to take a sip.

At that moment a slave came in carrying a gladius. Lucius recognised it instantly from the purplish-red stain on its tip. The slave handed it to Eumenes, who put down the tweezers and the sponge, wiped his hands on his apron, and picked up the gladius. He examined the tip closely for a long time. Then he rubbed the stained area with his fingertip and licked it.

Lucius gave a start of surprise.

Eumenes made a smacking noise with his lips as if he had just tasted a very expensive wine. 'Blood,' he declared.

'Blood?' cried Lucius.

'That's all it is. Some sort of animal, I think. It's not poisonous, I assure you.'

'So he'll be all right, then?'

'He'll be fine, Lucius. Don't worry.'

Eumenes went back to work on Quin's leg. He threaded some flax through a long iron needle and began suturing the wound. Quin bit his lip and cursed loudly through the pain.

Meanwhile Lucius sat back on his chair and let a big smile spread across his face. *Just blood!*

Crassus picked up the gladius. 'That fellow Crito was from the Neronian school in Capua, wasn't he?'

he muttered. 'One of their rituals is to slaughter a chicken before each fight and leave the blood on the blade. That must be what it is.'

Quin uttered another groan. His body was glistening with sweat; his breathing had become strained. Lucius went over to him. 'Don't worry, Quin,' he said, stroking his brother's damp hair. 'You're going to be all right.'

'Water!' croaked Quin.

Lucius fetched some and let a few drops pour onto his lips, which were dry and cracked. Quin licked it greedily, and Lucius let him swallow some more.

Eumenes was staring at Quin and frowning. He opened one of his patient's eyelids. 'Dilated pupils,' he murmured. 'Dry mouth, perspiration, laboured breathing... That wasn't poison on the sword, and yet...' He looked up sharply. 'Show me that blade again, Crassus.'

The lanista handed it over, and Eumenes examined it in the light of a pendant oil lamp. He shook his head. 'No, it's definitely blood. Quintus must have been poisoned by some other means.' He looked around the room until his eye fell on the goblet containing the mandrake potion.

Lucius felt threads of icy fear enter his blood as Eumenes marched over and picked up the goblet. He sniffed it. 'By Asclepius!'* cried the doctor. 'Who gave this to you, Lucius?'

*Asclepius: because Eumenes is Greek, he swears by the Greek god of medicine (known to the Romans as Aesculapius).

'Th– the slave,' stammered Lucius. 'The boy in the kitchen.'

'What boy?' cried Eumenes. 'The slave I told to prepare the potion was a girl!'

He dashed from the room, closely followed by Lucius and Crassus. The kitchen was empty when they got there. They found the slave girl's body in the storeroom next door. Her throat had been cut.

Quin was taken by carriage back to the Schola Armatorum, where he was given his own private bedroom. It was the last day of the games and the other visiting troupes had already departed, so the Schola felt a lot quieter and emptier.

Lucius kept vigil by Quin's bedside. He didn't let go of his brother's hand, even when Quin's grip became excruciatingly tight. In the light from the moon, Lucius could see Quin's powerful chest and arm muscles clench, his face a rictus of agony. Sweat pooled in the hollows of his neck and stomach and drenched the mattress.

Outside, the streets echoed with the Vulcanalia festivities. Lucius wished he could block out the drunken whoops and raucous singing of the revellers, but he needed the window open so the night breeze could keep his brother cool. He was overcome by a wave of bitterness towards this wretched city and its people. Their outrage at Crito's dastardly act had been brief and murderous, but had not extended to concern for the health of the victim. And now they had nothing on their minds except pleasure-seeking. It was no wonder that a ruthless criminal like Valens could prosper in a place like Pompeii!

As the hours passed, Quin's fever worsened. He tossed and turned and began to babble nonsense. Lucius dabbed his forehead with a damp towel, wishing he could do more. What could the gods possibly have had in mind – saving his brother in the arena, only to let him die so much more slowly and painfully from poison? Was this some divine joke? And the worst part of it was that *he*, Lucius, had given Quin the poison! Why hadn't he suspected the boy who'd prepared it? He should have known by now the levels of deceit and ruthlessness to which Valens would stoop to get his way.

Exhausted by the events of the day, Lucius began to nod off. At some point during the night, he thought he heard another of those gigantic, earth-shaking thuds, and then another, even louder – as if Vulcan himself were striding slowly across the Campanian Plain towards Pompeii.

CHAPTER X

4 hours before the eruption

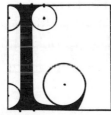

Lucius was roughly shaken awake. He opened his eyes and was momentarily blinded by the glare of morning sunlight from the window. Then he made out Ravilla's dark silhouette looming over him. From the direction of the bed he could hear Quin mumbling to himself.

'What do you know about me and Valens?' Ravilla was demanding, his face flushed with rage.

'What do you mean?' croaked Lucius, stalling.

'Quintus has been babbling about me and Valens and blackmail. He could only have got it from you. You were at Valens's house. Did you overhear something you weren't supposed to?'

He shook Lucius again, turning his world into a dizzying blur. But Lucius was determined to stay quiet. He carried within him the precious nugget of information that could save his father. If Ravilla even suspected that Lucius knew his secret, he would have the boy killed without hesitation. Lucius's only hope was to feign ignorance.

'I don't know what you mean, Uncle. I didn't hear anything.'

'Well, where does he get all this from, then?'

'I've no idea. It's probably just nonsense. He's hallucinating.'

Lucius shook off Ravilla's hand. He got up and went to look at his brother. Quin was hot to the touch and the pulse in his neck was very fast. He had his arm clamped tight over his eyes as if to block out the light.

'Eumenes told me he wouldn't last the night,' commented Ravilla.

'Well, he has,' said Lucius vehemently. 'And that has to be a hopeful sign.'

'He's strong, I grant you,' said Ravilla. 'But Quintus won't live to see the Tiber* again. You'd best get used to that fact.'

Ravilla was about to leave when something made him stop in his tracks. His eyes widened and his face stiffened into wariness. Lucius turned to see what had caused this change in his demeanour, and was

---

* *Tiber: the river that flows through Rome.*

surprised to see Atia standing in the doorway. She was staring at Lucius. Her bright eyes shimmered like pools of mercury.

'My dreams are clearer now,' she cried. 'The end of days is come. There will be darkness. Darkness in the midst of the day. I have seen a rain of stones, so thick it will turn the air solid. I have seen a crescent of fire that will cut us down like a bright sword. Pompeii will be destroyed today. On this day, I swear, Pompeii will be destroyed – in fire and in ash.'

'Today?' rasped Ravilla. 'What will bring this about?'

Atia pointed a trembling finger towards the window. Lucius and Ravilla both turned to look. There, in the distance, above the red-tiled roofs of the villas and the patchwork of vineyards, rose the dark, tapering form of Vesuvius. Lucius noticed that the summit was smoking, and there were more of those strange white streaks around it.

'That mountain will destroy Pompeii?' frowned Ravilla.

Atia nodded solemnly. Lucius recalled that Strabo, the Greek geographer, had suggested in his book that fire had once burned on the summit of Vesuvius. Could the same thing be happening again now?

'At noon today,' said Atia. 'I have seen it in my dreams. But I shall not see it with my eyes, for I will be dead before then. Escape while you still can.' She backed away from them. 'Now I must go and warn my master.'

'Wait!' said Lucius. 'What if you don't die? What if we keep you alive? Maybe none of this needs to happen.'

'I told you before,' said Atia, her eyes flickering fearfully towards Ravilla. 'My dreams are never wrong.'

With these words, she turned and ran off.

Ravilla immediately moved to follow her; but, before leaving, he turned back to Lucius. 'Tell Crassus to prepare the gladiators for immediate departure. I'll be back shortly.'

'Where are you going?' asked Lucius.

'I have some private business to attend to.'

Puzzled, Lucius watched his uncle stride quickly away. He found Crassus in bed – like Lucius, he'd not slept much. When Lucius passed on Ravilla's instruction, Crassus looked pleased.

'I don't like this city,' he growled. 'I don't like the big ground-thuds we've been hearing, nor the smell of the water. I especially don't like what happened to Quin! How is he, by the way?'

'Alive,' said Lucius.

Crassus nodded. 'Well, that's something.' He stretched and got out of bed. 'Go and tell Piso to fetch our wagons, will you?'

Lucius nodded and left. Before carrying out this order, however, he headed for Eumenes's quarters, intending to ask him to check on Quin. He met the doctor in the corridor, coming the other way.

'How's Quintus?' Eumenes asked, without breaking his stride.

'He survived, Doctor!' said Lucius, turning around and scurrying after him.

'Good!' said Eumenes.

'So there's hope, right?'

Eumenes stopped and turned, his lips trembling. 'Your brother is strong – we already knew that. But I know of no one who has survived as large a dose of belladonna as he received. You must be brave, Lucius, and prepare yourself for the worst.'

Lucius felt these words like a stab in the guts. 'We're leaving today,' he said. 'I– I want my mother and sister to see him… before he dies.'

'I think it most unlikely that he will survive the journey back to Rome,' said Eumenes gently. 'But you and I will travel in the litter with him. We will make him as comfortable as possible. You can tell your family of his exploits in the arena. Your brother is a hero. They should be proud of him.'

Lucius spent the next few hours helping to pack up the wagons. He carried out his duties mechanically, preoccupied as he was with thoughts of his brother. The sun was approaching its zenith as Lucius loaded up the last of the supplies. All that remained was to help Quin into the litter.

The air was hot and deathly still as he walked back towards the Schola Armatorum. The city was quiet, its people in their homes, some perhaps still sleeping off the previous night's revelries. The atmosphere felt dense and heavy, yet somehow fragile, like a bubble about to burst.

Suddenly his path was blocked by Ravilla. 'Are we ready?' his uncle asked, looking agitatedly at something beyond Lucius's head. 'Remember, we must be gone by midday.'

Lucius had been so concerned with Quin, he'd forgotten about Atia's prediction. 'I need to fetch my brother,' he said, sidestepping Ravilla. As he did so, he noticed something red on his uncle's toga. It looked like a smear of blood. A horrid thought struck him.

'Where is Atia?' he asked urgently.

'How would I know?' said Ravilla impatiently. 'More to the point, where's Crassus? We should be leaving by now.'

'What have you done with Atia?' Lucius demanded.

Lucius was suddenly sure that Ravilla had killed her. He'd silenced her before she could pass on her warning to Valens, so that Valens would remain in Pompeii and die in the coming devastation. Of course, all knowledge of Ravilla's big secret would die with him – or so Ravilla thought.

Ravilla tried a reassuring smile, but he wasn't as talented as Valens at concealing his true feelings, and the panicked look in his eyes betrayed him.

'Atia is fine,' he said. 'The girl is a complete faker, of course. She made up that story about me and Aquila – you know, that one about the Tarpeian Rock. Complete fiction.'

'Then why are you so concerned that we leave by midday?' asked Lucius, fixing him with a steely look. 'If she's a faker, what's the hurry?'

Ravilla uttered a nervous laugh. 'Well, it's best not to take any chances, you know!'

Crassus emerged from the building's entrance at the head of a line of gladiators. 'We're all ready for the off, sir,' reported the lanista.

'Good,' said Ravilla. 'We must be out of here in the next five minutes.'

'Very good, sir.'

Lucius was now worried that Ravilla would insist on leaving before Quin had been fetched from his bed. He moved towards the Schola entrance, but before he could reach it he felt someone grab his arm.

'You are Lucius, yes?' asked a slave, breathless from running.

'Yes.'

'I have a message for you. From Eprius.'

Lucius took the scroll he was handed. As he did so, he noticed his hand was shaking. There was a vibration coming from beneath the street, deep down in the earth. He could hear a rumbling that grew steadily louder with each second.

Another earthquake!

The horses attached to the wagons behind him started to whinny. Boxes, just loaded, tumbled to the ground. The earth itself was trembling, sending up thin clouds of dust. A boom rolled across the plain, followed immediately by another, and Lucius was almost knocked off his feet by a sudden scorching blast of air.

One of the gladiators shouted: 'Look at that!'

He was pointing at Vesuvius.

Something monstrous had happened to the mountain. At first it seemed as though a gigantic, brawny fist had smashed its way through the summit. A dense, brown, unimaginably tall column was rising straight up from the mountaintop into the cloudless blue sky. Narrow at its base, it gradually widened as it rose until, at its apex, it fanned outwards. It reminded Lucius of the branches of a tree, only he could see that the trunk of this colossal tree was not solid, but a thundering, boiling mass of violent upward movement. The branches at the top split and split again into millions of slender brown tendrils that spread out across the sky, then curved slowly downwards, dissolving at their edges into a fine, falling mist.

The end of days is come, thought Lucius calmly. The messenger boy had collapsed to his knees and was shielding his face from the sky, mumbling entreaties to the gods. Many of the gladiators had fled back indoors. One had untethered a horse and was galloping wildly eastwards, heading for the Sarno Gate. Ravilla was shouting orders at Crassus, but it was hard to hear him above the deafening rumble. Crassus ignored him anyway. He simply stared at Vesuvius.

When Lucius looked back towards the mountain, he could no longer see it. Now the whole view to the north was a dense brown, rolling fog that was advancing rapidly towards them across the plain. It was like one of the sandstorms described so vividly by Quintus Numidicus in his North African chronicles.

Within seconds, the storm had hit the northern suburbs of Pompeii, and Lucius could see that it was made not of sand but of rocks. The rocks tumbled so thickly, they seemed like a single, solid, churning mass, engulfing the city and everything else from horizon to horizon. The coming storm cloaked everything it passed over, blocking it from sight. At its leading edge, Lucius saw thousands of individual rocks bounce off red roofs and pediments, pummelling trees and knocking statues from their pedestals.

The street Lucius was standing in was suddenly full of people fleeing, either to the south, or west towards the harbour. Lucius was jostled, spun around and nearly knocked over as hundreds of panicked citizens surged past him. The falling rocks were coming closer all the time – they were just a few blocks away now. Crassus was pushing the remaining gladiators back into the Schola. Ravilla, evidently realising that escape from Pompeii was now impossible, followed him inside. Lucius dragged the cowering messenger boy to

177

his feet and hauled him towards the entrance. They dashed into the vestibule just as the first rocks began to rain down on the street outside.

Crassus slammed the door shut. The noise outside and above was a continuous, thunderous, clattering roar. The walls were visibly trembling and drifts of plaster dust fell from the ceiling. The lanista stared fearfully upwards. 'How long before the roof collapses?' he asked no one in particular.

Piso, the head slave, was sweeping up the remains of a bust that had fallen from its plinth. 'The roof of this building is strong, sir,' he assured Crassus. 'We will be safe in here.'

'The Schola is new,' added Gaius Calidius, the building's manager. 'It was built after the earthquake, and it's withstood every storm and ground tremor since then.'

'Sorry if I don't share your optimism,' said Ravilla scornfully, 'but this is hardly your average storm or ground tremor.'

Calidius bowed his head.

'Is there a basement?' Ravilla asked.

'No, I'm afraid there isn't.'

'Well, which is the sturdiest room here?' asked Crassus.

Calidius thought about this. 'The armoury, I should think.'

He led the way towards the back of the building, followed by Ravilla, Crassus, and all the gladiators and slaves. Meanwhile, Lucius went to Quin's room. It was dark except for the faint glow of an oil lamp. The window had been shuttered, but through the slats he glimpsed the dense and continuous rockfall. Eumenes was sitting on the edge of Quin's bed with a goblet in his hand. Quin was delirious, tossing and turning, ranting nonsense words.

'Hold him still, will you?' said Eumenes.

It took all of Lucius's strength to hold down his brother's powerful, heaving shoulders while Eumenes poured the medicinal potion into his parched mouth.

'This contains valerian root,' explained Eumenes. 'It should keep him calm during these final stages of his life.' He looked towards the window. 'What manner of storm is this?'

'Rocks falling from the sky,' said Lucius, keeping his eyes on Quin. 'They're coming out of Vesuvius.'

They heard a sound directly above their heads like a cracking of timbers, and dust began to fall in alarming quantities.

'We have to get out him of here,' said Lucius. 'Everyone's in the armoury. Calidius thinks it's the safest place.'

Together they lifted Quin onto a stretcher, then hurriedly left the room, just as a huge timber crashed down onto the floor amid a fog of dust. They walked as fast as they could up the corridor. Through a doorway to the right, Lucius glimpsed the devastated training arena, the only part of the building open to the elements. A falling cloud of rocks thundered down onto the arena floor, which had disappeared beneath a rapidly deepening layer of pale brown stones.

The armoury was not small. Yet, with everyone in the building – some forty people in total – crowded in there, it seemed cramped. A row of wooden cabinets containing armour and weapons lined the long wall at the back of the room. Space was quickly made for Quin on a bench fixed to the opposite wall. He seemed calmer now, thankfully. Lucius seated himself on the floor close to his brother.

The rockfall was an unrelenting, pounding rattle above them. The gladiators, usually a lively group, were muted. Everyone was too stunned to know what to say. There were frequent anxious glances at the ceiling, but – so far, at least – this part of the roof seemed to be holding firm under the barrage. Ravilla looked nervous and jumpy, continuously getting up from his chair and pacing around, or engaging in whispered conferences with Crassus or Calidius.

Lucius's eye fell on the messenger, who was still on his knees praying. In all the confusion, Lucius had completely forgotten about the scroll with the message from Eprius! He took it out of his pocket. It carried the seal of the Domitii, Eprius's family. Lucius unfurled it. The message was very short, and the uneven handwriting suggested it had been written in a hurry. It read:

My dear Lucius,

I have made an important discovery. I know where your father is. Come to Valens's house as soon as you can. Marcipor is expecting you and will let you in. I will meet you in the courtyard by the Neptune fountain. Then I will tell you everything.

Your friend, Eprius

Lucius shook inside when he read the words 'I know where your father is'. If he had been able to, he would have run straight to Valens's house that minute. He had to get there   but how? He would be killed instantly if he stepped outside this building now. But surely these rocks couldn't go on falling for ever. At some point they had to stop. He could only hope that he and Eprius would still be alive by the time that happened.

The hours crawled by – Lucius wasn't sure how many. The bombardment outside continued without cessation, and it seemed to Lucius that the entire innards of the Earth were being emptied out onto Pompeii. With the sun and sky hidden by the stony storm, it was impossible to tell the time of day. The gladiators tried to keep their spirits up by singing. Some tried telling jokes, but the laughter that greeted these sounded harsh and forced. Cold meat, bread and water were retrieved from the kitchen. Crassus made sure that the rations were doled out fairly and equally to everyone. Quin slept through most of this,

his breathing jagged, his skin permanently bathed in sweat. Lucius gave Quin most of his water ration.

At some point, shortly after their meal, there came a terrifying bang from outside the room, followed by a ripping sound, as if the entire fabric of the building was being torn asunder. Crassus opened the door. 'The ceiling is splitting all along the corridor!' he yelled. He slammed the door shut just as a cloud of brown dust blew into the room.

'We'll be safe in here, I assure you!' vowed Calidius, though Lucius now detected a whine of fear in his tone.

Less than a minute after he had said this, a giant crack appeared above the doorway, sending a cloud of dust spiralling down. Everyone stared at the crack as it spread jerkily through the plaster, spidering outwards until most of the ceiling had splintered.

'By the gods!' groaned Ravilla. 'We're doomed!'

There followed a hideous, creaking, rupturing sound, and then half the ceiling fell in.

A gladiator sitting next to Quin died instantly as a heavy wooden beam crashed down on his head. Others seated nearby disappeared beneath the thick brown cascade of dust and rock that poured through the hole. Lucius was bombarded by rocks and was surprised at how light they felt as they bounced off him. He dived towards Quin, who was already half-submerged beneath the roaring avalanche. But before he could reach him, the wall directly above his brother suddenly toppled forward. Time seemed to stand still for Lucius as he watched the wall, with its fresco of the winged goddess of victory, come falling down in one enormous chunk, entombing Quin beneath it. Lucius began pulling at the shattered brickwork of the wall, trying to reach Quin, but he felt himself weakening, losing consciousness, as the rocks battered him incessantly. Hands grasped him, pulling him back.

CHAPTER XI

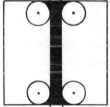n what remained of the armoury, Lucius lay in a daze on the floor, caked in yellowish-brown dust. One whole side of the room, nearest the door, had disappeared beneath the rockfall. Twenty people were buried under there, including Quin. He had lost his brother!

The remainder of the ceiling formed an irregular-shaped ledge that was somehow withstanding the rain of stones, and the survivors gathered beneath its meagre shelter. Ravilla was among them. He had climbed into one of the wooden cabinets on the back wall and was cowering inside it. Crassus was distributing helmets and shields to the others for protection in case the rest of the ceiling caved in.

Lucius barely noticed any of this, nor did he feel the bruises that now covered his body where the rocks had hit him. He was staring at the blurry curtain of stony rain that now formed the fourth wall of the room.

Quin was gone!

He felt Eumenes's hand on his shoulder. 'At least he died quickly,' the doctor said gently. 'Better than lingering on as the poison did its work.'

Lucius picked up one of the stones that had fallen near his foot. He turned it over in his hands. It was about the size of a child's fist, and full of tiny holes.

'These stones are so light,' he said to Eumenes. 'It looks like a sponge made out of stone.'

Eumenes chuckled at this description. 'It's pumice,' he said. 'It's full of air bubbles. They used it to make the domes of the famous baths at Baiae, because it's so light... But there's no hope for your brother, I'm afraid. Nor any of those other poor souls underneath there. No one could survive a pummelling like that.

Lucius continued to stare at the deepening mound under which his brother lay buried. Was it his imagination, or was the storm of stones easing slightly?

'Hey, it's stopping!' cried one of the gladiators.

The thunderous noise began to diminish, and the cataract of stones became more sporadic.

'I can see the mountain,' said another voice.

Lucius looked up through the clouds of yellowish-brown dust and saw, beyond the collapsed wall of their room, beyond the training arena and the broken roofs of Pompeii, the dark peak of Vesuvius. It looked different. The summit was flatter, with one side lower than the other.

As they watched, something very bright appeared at the lip of the lower side of the summit – a dazzling line of orange, shaped like a sinister, gloating smile. It spilled down the western slope of the mountain: a fast-moving, smoking, burning arc that left little spots of orange flame in its wake. Lucius instantly thought of Atia's prediction: *I have seen a crescent of fire that will cut us down like a bright sword.*

The stones had almost ceased falling now. A gladiator, with a helmet and shield to protect him, clambered up the great mound of stones that now filled the front half of the room. From the top, he watched the progress of the sickle-shaped line of flame.

'It's heading west,' he yelled. 'Straight for Herculaneum.'

Lucius immediately thought of his father. There had been a rumour that he was there.

'What is it?' someone cried.

The gladiator on the mound blinked and rubbed his eyes. 'I don't know,' he said. 'Something very hot – some kind of fiery river – straight out of the pits of Hades. Poor sods. It's moving so fast, they won't stand a chance in Herculaneum.'

It may not have been true that Father was there! Lucius told himself. *I am not going to lose my brother and my father in a single day!*

'We should use this opportunity to get out of here,' said Ravilla, emerging hesitantly from his cabinet. 'The stones aren't falling so heavily now. In our helmets and shields, we should be able to get through this.'

'Very good, sir,' said Crassus, staring at the mound of stones that lay between them and the rest of the Schola. 'How exactly do you propose we get out of here?'

'We can climb up a pile of these cabinets and then get out through the hole in the roof,' said Ravilla.

'Right!' said Crassus, looking pleased to have a job to do. He began issuing orders. Slaves and gladiators started ripping the cabinets from the walls and then piling them up to create a mound that they could use to climb towards the ceiling. Behind the cabinets there were more frescoes of winged victories carrying swords, shields, nets and spears. These reminded Lucius of the painting of the goddess that had fallen on top of Quin. A desperate idea flared in his mind.

'Part of the wall fell on top of him, just before the stones came down,' he murmured to Eumenes.

'What do you mean?' asked the doctor.

Without stopping to answer, Lucius grabbed an armoured breastplate and began using it like a shovel to dig into the mound of pumice.

'The part that fell is leaning against the part that's still standing,' he shouted as he worked. 'Quin was inside the angle. The wall may have protected him from the rocks. He may still be alive under there!'

Several gladiators stopped what they were doing when Lucius said this. They abandoned their tower-building and instead began digging rocks from the mound. After his impressive victories against the local gladiators, Quin was one of the most popular men in the familia. If there was any chance that he might still be alive, they would do whatever they could to rescue him.

'This is madness!' cried Ravilla. 'You're wasting time trying to dig out a corpse. We need to save ourselves. Quintus was almost dead from poisoning anyway, so what's the point?'

'You heard the man!' yelled Crassus. 'Now stop that at once and do as you're told!'

Maybe it was because oaths of loyalty didn't feel quite so important after all that had happened, or maybe it was because such oaths were outweighed by their loyalty to a trapped comrade, but not one of gladiators obeyed Crassus's order. In fact, more of them joined the endeavour, using cabinet doors, helmets, shields or whatever came to hand to dig through the mound.

Within twenty minutes, they had reached the broken chunk of wall. Lucius, with help from one of the gladiators, dragged the dust-shrouded Quin from the little gap in which he had lain.

He was very still when they laid him down on the floor, and Lucius began to fear the worst.

'Quin?' he whispered into his ear. 'It's Lucius. Can you hear me?'

Nothing.

Lucius began to cry, and a tear splashed on his brother's cheek, forming a little river through the dust.

Quin blinked, then coughed, expelling a cloud of yellow dust. A smile slowly formed on his face. 'Hey! Little brother!'

Lucius uttered a small scream of joy. He fell on Quin, hugging him hard. They gave him water, and cleaned the dust from his face and hair.

Eumenes examined him and pronounced it a medical miracle. 'Your brother is still weak, but he seems better – a lot better! There are no more symptoms of the poison.' Then he frowned and picked up one of the pumice stones. 'What was it you likened these to? A sponge made of stone. I wonder whether...'

'What?' coaxed Lucius.

'I've heard that pumice is highly absorbent – like a sponge. It's just possible that this is what saved him. Being buried in pumice might somehow have absorbed the poison. Who knows?'

'I can't remember much since the fight,' Quin said to Lucius. 'What's been going on?'

'Oh, nothing much,' chuckled Lucius. 'You were poisoned. And then the mountain exploded and you were buried alive beneath a hill of stones.'

'That's all?'

'That's all.'

'Who poisoned me?'

'I think it was someone working for Valens.'

Quin looked at him.

'He knew what you were planning to do, Quin. He has spies everywhere…'

Before they could continue this conversation, Crassus's voice boomed out: 'Right! Fun's over, lads! Back to work now! Let's get all these cabinets piled up.'

The miraculous survival and recovery of Quin had given the troupe a huge morale boost. Exhausted as they were, they willingly got on with the job of constructing a tower of cabinets. The tower was a precarious structure, and it collapsed a couple of times during the process, but eventually they managed to build it all the way up to the hole in the ceiling, where it met the remaining ledge of roof.

Ravilla sent his personal slave up first to test it. After he was safely up, Ravilla went next, then Eumenes, Crassus and Calidius, and finally the gladiators and slaves. Quin insisted on going up unaided, despite having the use of only one leg. Once Quin was safely up, Lucius made the climb himself. He let out a gasp when he took in the view at the top. The streets and buildings had all but disappeared and the entire city was submerged up to the level of the rooftops. It looked like a wild, rugged plain – no longer a city, but an undulating desert of stones. The air was clogged with brown, swirling dust that blew in his face and made him cough. Here and there through the gloom they could see the glow from the oil lamps of other survivors who must also have managed to climb out of their buried homes.

The rockfall started to grow in strength. The pumice clanged on Lucius's Murmillo helmet and pounded painfully on his back and shoulders. In his fist he carried Eprius's crumpled note.

'Come on!' called Ravilla. 'Let's move on out!'

'Which way?' queried Crassus. 'I've completely lost my bearings.'

Ravilla cast around trying to find some landmark. Then he caught sight of the still-burning fires on the mountain. 'Anywhere but there!' he cried.

Crassus organised everyone into a column facing the opposite way from Vesuvius. In the distance they glimpsed a hazy cluster of lights that may have been Stabiae or possibly Surrentum on the southern side of the bay – towns that were hopefully beyond the range of Vesuvius's fury. A couple of poles were fitted to a wooden chair to create a crude litter to transport Quin.

'Line up with the others, Lucius!' yelled Crassus.

'I'm not going!' Lucius shouted back. He couldn't leave Pompeii yet – not while there was a chance of finding out where his father was.

'By all the gods, why not?'

'I have to do something first.'

'Leave him!' cried Ravilla. 'If the boy is determined to die, let him.'

'Here!' said Crassus, offering Lucius a large Secutor's shield. 'Good luck, son!'

Lucius thanked him. He watched the column begin moving off into the darkness.

'Lucius!' called Quin, craning his neck to look back. 'What's going on?'

'Stay safe!' cried Lucius. 'I'll see you back in Rome!' Then, under his breath, he added: 'I love you, Quin.'

Lucius remembered that Valens's house was in the northwest of the city, north of the Forum. Vesuvius was due north of Pompeii, so he chose a route across the sea of stones a little way left of Vesuvius, hoping this would bring him more or less to the right part of town. The stones were pelting down at a fierce rate now, and he had to crouch beneath the shield for protection. Progress was very slow. With every step, he sank shin-deep in the pumice. Once or twice he lost his footing and tumbled down the slopes. Then he had to scramble hastily to his feet to avoid being buried beneath a fresh fall of stones. Here and there, under the eaves of roofs or beneath the tops of arches, he saw shadowy movements and the occasional flickering of a fire. So there was life in the city – it wasn't quite the end of days that Atia had predicted. But then he remembered that curving line of fire scything down the mountainside into Herculaneum, and he shuddered.

At length, the rockfall began to ease again. Soon after that, he saw the bright light appearing once again at the lip of the mountain's summit. Each appearance of the fiery crescent seemed to coincide with a diminishing in the rockfall, as if the mountain could not produce both at once.

He watched the burning cloud descend at a furious rate, but this time, to his horror, he saw that it was coming straight towards Pompeii! Beyond Vesuvius, the Campanian plain seemed to rear up like a great black shadow pulsing with inner fire. A wave of heat hit him in the face, carrying with it a terrible stench of sulphur and burning. The cloud billowed upwards like a second mountain and seemed about to engulf the northern edge of the city. Then it subsided and its radiance faded, leaving only a sprinkling of little fires that marked its passage down the mountainside. The deadly wave had spent itself, thank the gods, before it could reach the city. But next time the people of Pompeii might not be so lucky. He had to find Eprius quickly, before they both perished.

But after another half-hour of struggling through the stones, Lucius was close to exhaustion. Each step had become excruciating. The strain of moving his legs through the loose piles of pumice, the weight of his shield, the bruising all over his body, had all taken its toll, and all he wanted to do was to go to sleep. To fall down among these soft, light stones, to feel them fall like gentle rain on top of him, to be buried in them like a warm cocoon – that was a very tempting prospect.

He had no idea where he was. Every rooftop looked the same. He could keep going to the very limits of the city and never find Valens's house. For all he knew, he could be passing over it right now. He wished he'd paid more attention to the building's roof design. Did it have a distinctive ornamentation, or a tower? He had no idea, and he wondered how he ever thought he could find his way back there.

Finally, Lucius came to a halt. The stones were falling more heavily again. He crouched beneath his shield, feeling the pumice build up around his thighs, and accepting in his heart that he'd failed. He remained there for a long time, half-deafened by the drumming of the rocks on his shield. He knew he should try to look for some shelter, but his body, now it had stopped, seemed unable to start moving again. He looked around, hoping to find a roof with people under it – people who might possibly be able to help him find his way. But there were no people in sight. Instead, his attention was caught by something very odd right in front of him. It looked like the top of an iron-barred cage – it must be a very tall cage to rise so high above the level of the stones. With a rush of excitement, he realised what it was: the cage belonging to that African animal, the one with the long neck, in Valens's zoo. Somehow, he'd found Valens's house! He looked around him, and soon he began to recognise other features: the top of the peristyle colonnade, and the smaller roof surrounding the courtyard.

He quickly dug himself out of the mound of stones now rising around him, and began crawling back towards the front of the house.

He came to the atrium with the hole in the roof above the pool. The stones had piled up to about a metre below the level of the ceiling, and a short, easy jump took him inside the house. Oil lamps flickered in the shadows below him. So there was life in here! In the glow of these lamps, he saw that he was standing on the summit of a small pumice mountain, whose base extended almost to the edges of the expansive atrium floor. He carefully edged his way down the steep flank of the mountain. His hesitant descent quickly turned into an uncontrolled slide and then a chaotic tumble amid a minor avalanche of pumice. He landed face down on the floor, his body by now feeling like one big bruise.

With a groan, Lucius looked up to see where he was, and found himself near the entrance to the tablinum. The roof had partially collapsed here. A great, dusty mound of roof beams, tiles and pumice blocked off access to Valens's private study. Perhaps the master of the house was dead – Ravilla had prevented Atia from warning him of the danger. Well, if anyone deserved to perish today, it was Valens. Lucius imagined him dying alone in his little lair, surrounded by his scrolls full of other people's secrets, realising that all the money he'd extorted from his victims over the years was ultimately worth nothing.

Yet some people must still be alive here – there were lamps burning in the recesses of the remaining portion of the room. Lucius prayed that the survivors included Eprius. There was no sound, except for the steady thunder of rocks above his head. He saw a flicker of light in the passageway that led to the kitchen. Perhaps he would find people there. He climbed unsteadily to his feet and hobbled across the room and down the corridor. When he reached the kitchen he peered in, then jerked backwards in shock.

Lying on the floor was Atia. There was blood on her tunic, and her extraordinary silvery-blue eyes were now still and lifeless. They would see no more mysteries. Lucius knelt down and closed them.

'Little Atia,' he whispered. 'You saw all this. You could have saved yourself – couldn't you?'

He reflected for a moment on the short, yet amazing life of this little girl. She had been born for a special purpose – she knew what it was, and was content to fulfil it and then die. For most people, himself included, life was a continuous, unfolding mystery, and the hardest part was to work out what one's own role should be.

Lucius was conscious that time was slipping away. The crescent of fire would return, as Atia had predicted, and this time it would sweep right over Pompeii. He had to find Eprius quickly and learn what he'd discovered, and then the two of them could make their escape.

He walked over to the doorway on the far side of the kitchen and peered through it. The roof had collapsed in the passageway, blocking access to the slaves' quarters beyond. Returning to the tablinum, Lucius noticed that the peristyle was inaccessible from there, but could be reached by climbing through the window in the triclinium – the colonnade had partially survived the bombardment, possibly allowing access to the rear part of the house.

He entered the triclinium and eased himself through the window into the peristyle. The garden was, of course, buried under three metres of pumice, and all that remained of the surrounding colonnade was a narrow passage close to the wall, already filling up with stones. Oil lamps had been placed on the window ledges along the wall, almost like guides to a trail. This way, he was sure, he would find the remaining members of the household, whoever they might be.

He followed the peristyle as it bent to the right, then continued as far as the entrance to the marble-floored hall on his left. There were lamps burning in here and also in the equipment room adjoining the bath-house, whose door stood ajar. It was to the furnace room that lay beneath there that Eprius had taken him two nights ago.

Of course! It must have been Eprius who had laid the oil-lamp trail. He was leading Lucius back to their secret meeting place! His heart beating faster now, Lucius ran across the hall, then along the length of the equipment room and down the narrow spiral steps at the end. He removed his helmet and crouched as he passed into the low-ceilinged furnace room. By the light of the fire burning in the brazier, he was overjoyed to see his friend Eprius.

But then his eyes took in the three people with him, seated on stools or baskets in the cramped underground space. There was Marcipor the porter, and the tall, thin boy who had poisoned Quin the previous night... And there was Valens.

CHAPTER XII

elcome, Lucius!' smiled Valens. 'We've been expecting you!'

Lucius stared at him, aghast. He thought of the oil lamps laid out like a trail, leading him down to this room. Was this whole thing a trap?

'As you can see, my household is somewhat diminished at present,' continued Valens, 'as is my ability to offer you my customary level of hospitality, but we have a little wooden box all ready for you here. Please do sit down.'

'You were expecting me?' spluttered Lucius, remaining on his feet. He turned to his friend. 'What's going on, Eprius?'

Eprius bowed his head, not meeting his eyes.

'I'm sorry, Lucius. He forced me to write that note. He was going to tell my parents everything if I didn't.'

'Do you know where my father is?' cried Lucius.

Eprius looked up, then shook his head, his eyes full of tears. 'I'm so sorry to have given you hope.'

'The lure worked,' chuckled Valens. 'And here you are, as I knew you would be. Not even a blizzard of stones is enough to keep you from your quest to find your beloved father.'

Lucius tried to get his breathing under control. 'Why?' he shouted at Valens. 'Why did you bring me here?'

'I should have thought it was quite obvious,' said Valens placidly. 'You overheard my conversation with your uncle the other night, then blabbed about it to your brother and Crassus. I can't tolerate that sort of behaviour, Lucius. Much as I like you, I have certain responsibilities to my clients. I vowed to Ravilla that I would protect his secret. I wasn't worried so much about your telling Crassus. He's part of my protected circle, and his loyalty to Ravilla virtually guarantees his discretion. Your brother, however, was a different kind of beast. Hot-headed, prone to emotional outbursts – I'm afraid I had no choice but to kill him.'

'Well, he survived,' smiled Lucius.

Valens raised his eyebrows and glanced at the tall, thin boy. The boy shook his head. 'He's lying,' he insisted. 'His brother drank enough of that stuff to kill a horse.'

'Quintus is dead,' said Valens mildly. 'Accept it, Lucius. And accept also that you must share the same fate. I'm afraid I simply can't trust you. You're too much like your father – virtuous to a fault.'

'You told me that my father taught you about virtue,' said Lucius. 'Was that another of your lies?'

'Not at all,' chuckled Valens. 'Your father was a great teacher – though the lesson I learned from him may not have been the one he intended to teach. He taught me that virtue has nothing to do with status or appearance – a noble exterior too often hides a wicked heart. In his investigations here, he exposed many a villain among the most respected in our community. For your father, the answer was to punish them and thereby create a more virtuous society. But I saw different possibilities. With all this villainy secretly bubbling away beneath the surface of our public life, why expose it? Far better to profit from it. Your father would never have understood that, and I can tell that you can't either – I'm sorry about that, and I'm sorry that it means that you will have to die.'

He nodded at the tall, thin boy. 'Albinus, it is time.'

The boy rose to his feet, stooping to avoid the low ceiling, and drew a knife from his belt. Lucius backed away from him, tripping on the lowest step of the spiral stairway and falling onto his back.

'Wait!' cried Lucius, shrugging off the boy's attempt to grab hold of him. 'Think, Valens! Why are you doing this? We're all going to die here anyway!'

'Nonsense!' said Valens sharply. 'We will rebuild this town. We did it before, after the earthquake. Pompeii will rise again!'

Albinus now had Lucius in his clutches. He pulled him to his feet and placed the edge of the blade close to Lucius's neck.

'Have you seen what's happening up there?' cried Lucius desperately. 'There are waves of fire sweeping down the mountain, incinerating everything in their path. Herculaneum is already destroyed. One of them will soon hit Pompeii. This city is doomed, and we are, too, if we stay here!'

'Shall I kill him now?' growled the boy.

Valens was no longer smiling. He stood up and came very close to Lucius. He pointed up the stairwell and whispered: 'While that little girl lives, Pompeii will survive. That's what she told us.'

Lucius stared at him, eyes popping from his head. 'Then you don't know?'

'I'll kill him!' shrieked Albinus, and Lucius felt the sharpness of the blade pressing into his throat.

'Wait!' yelled Valens, pulling back the boy's arm. '*What* don't I know?'

'Atia is dead!' said Lucius.

'What?' cried Valens, his face paling. 'You're lying!'

'I found her body in the kitchen,' murmured Lucius. 'Ravilla killed her.'

'Is this true?' demanded Valens, seizing Albinus by the collar and pushing him against the wall.

'Y– yes, sir,' admitted Albinus.

'Why wasn't I told?'

'I didn't want to upset you, sir.'

Valens pushed him to the ground.

'We have to go now!' said Lucius.

Valens didn't move. He was staring at the fire. Eventually he turned and faced the others: 'We're not leaving,' he said flatly. 'If we go up there, we could be hit by the wave of fire as we try to escape. We'll be safe down here. Let Vesuvius do its worst. These walls are thick.' He nodded towards some baskets in the corner of the room. 'We have enough food and water for a few days. When the mountain's fury is spent, we'll dig ourselves out. We'll move to another city and start again. Maybe to Rome. There's plenty of potential profit for the likes of me in that nest of vipers.'

He went and sat down on his stool. 'For now, we stay here!'

Lucius made for the stairwell. 'You stay if you wish!' he said. 'I'm leaving.' He turned. 'Eprius, are you coming?'

Eprius looked uncertain. He glanced sheepishly at Valens.

'I thought I had made myself clear,' said Valens. 'Eprius is not going anywhere, and neither are you.'

'Why do you care?' Lucius challenged him.

'I care because if, by some miracle, you do survive, Lucius, I don't want you going around telling everyone

Ravilla's secret – he may be my only surviving client, after all.'

Lucius shot him a hateful look. He grabbed Eprius's arm and pulled him up from his box. 'Come on!'

'Stop them, Marcipor!' ordered Valens.

The big, fair-haired porter stood in front of the stairwell, blocking the way.

'If you want to survive this, Marcipor, come with us,' said Lucius.

The porter didn't move.

'Come with us,' said Eprius softly.

Lucius turned in surprise. Eprius was breathing quickly. His eyes were still fearful but they possessed a glittering hardness Lucius hadn't seen before.

'Do you care for your life, Eprius?' snarled Valens.

'I don't think so!' answered the boy. 'It's not much of a life, is it, Valens? Not since I met you, anyway.'

Marcipor's normally impassive face was now frowning uncertainly.

'I am your master, Marcipor,' said Valens, his voice a mixture of velvet and steel. 'You will obey me.'

Marcipor appeared to hesitate for a moment, then he moved aside. 'My place is here, with my master,' he said to Eprius. 'But you go. Enjoy your life, my friend.'

Lucius began running up the steps. He could hear Eprius coming up behind him.

'Stop them!' echoed Valens's voice from below, but Marcipor must have blocked any attempt by Albinus to obey this order.

They ran through the equipment room and out into the hallway beyond, then picked their way as quickly as they could through the broken remains of the peristyle. Very soon they were back in the atrium, where they launched themselves at the mountain of pumice that would take them up to the roof. It was very hard to gain purchase on the slope, as the stones kept slipping and tumbling beneath their hands and feet, but after several attempts the pair neared the top of the mound. By this time, the pumice pile had reached almost to the very top of the ceiling, leaving them a tiny gap to squeeze through.

Finally, they emerged onto the roof, and Eprius gasped when he took in the changed landscape. He flinched and cried out as the stones pelted him. 'Here,' cried Lucius, handing him the shield. 'Put this over your head.'

'Which way?' yelled Eprius from under the shield.

Navigating from the fires on Vesuvius, Lucius swivelled himself to a position that he thought must face the harbour. 'This way to the sea!' he called. 'We can try and take a ship!'

Eprius nodded, and the two boys – one in a Murmillo's helmet, the other crouching beneath a Secutor's shield – began wading through the stones.

They moved slowly through the dusky brown wasteland. Lightning flashed above them and in its glow they picked out, here and there, the huddled shapes of people travelling in the same direction – and that gave Lucius hope that they were indeed heading for the harbour. Another shimmer of lightning lit the underside of the clouds ahead of them, revealing in silhouette the city wall and its watchtowers. A series of pillars stuck up like broken teeth – the remains of a temple, perhaps?

They sensed growing numbers of people around them as they neared the base of the city wall. A low-roofed tunnel loomed out of the twilight, and they saw it was the nearly buried remains of one of Pompeii's great arched gateways. Its vaulted roof now rose less than a metre above their heads. They were shouldered roughly aside as lines of pedestrian traffic converged on this single exit point. But eventually Lucius and Eprius managed to join the general flow of refugees into the tunnel. Shouts and complaints echoed loudly in the congested darkness as people were jostled or trodden on.

The boys emerged at the top of a gentle slope. Lucius squinted into the dusty gloom, trying to make out the harbour. He could hear the sound of waves in the distance and could make out shapes in the pumice that might be wharves and quaysides – but where was the sea? With a shock, he realised he was looking at it. The masts of ships stuck up through the stones like the drowning arms of sailors. The pumice storm had covered even the sea – the stones were so light, they floated! There was no chance of an escape from the city by ship.

There were groans of despair as this awareness dawned on the people around them. The crowd gradually dispersed, some to the north, heading up the coast towards Herculaneum, others south, and still others turned back the way they had come. Lucius, recalling that Crassus had led the gladiators southwards, decided to join the refugees heading in that direction. At some point they must have crossed the River Sarnus, submerged like everything else by the blanket of stones. As they walked, Lucius noticed that the hail of pumice was easing once more. This provoked several sighs of relief from those around them.

'It seems to be easing,' panted Eprius.

'Come on!' said Lucius, quickening his pace. 'This means the mountain's getting ready to spit out another of those fiery surges.'

'I don't know if I can go any further,' gasped Eprius.

Lucius gave him a worried glance. The boy looked done in, barely able to raise his knees above the stones to keep going.

'You go on!' Eprius told him. 'I'll be fine here.'

Lucius tried pulling him forward, but he, too, was close to exhaustion, and found himself subsiding back into the stones. He looked back towards the city walls and the flickering torches of the lost souls now wandering the ruins. He looked beyond, towards the fire-speckled crest of Vesuvius, rising above the city like a brooding titan.

Perhaps we'll be safe here, he thought. *We may be far enough.*

As Lucius watched, he saw a cloudy star appear on the mountain peak. The star swelled and deepened to a rosy orange flecked with black, then tipped out of the cavernous mouth like a giant lolling tongue. It seemed to expand as it rolled down the side of the mountain. As it advanced, it curved into a merciless smile. It was coming straight for them, as Lucius knew it would.

I have seen a crescent of fire that will cut us down like a bright sword.

The incandescent wave raced down the mountain into the plain. It was a grey, seething mass pulsing with orange, like a glowing cloud, and it moved faster than anything imaginable as it closed in on the city. Lucius watched it strike the northern walls and crash upwards like a breaking wave of flame and foaming gas. He saw walls shatter and roofs explode before it. He saw tiny black specks, that might be people, hurled backwards. The frothing tide rolled through the city, smothering it in a carpet of smoke and flame, engulfing and obliterating everything in its path. Lucius thought of Valens, Albinus and Marcipor, cooked alive in their little hideout beneath the ground. He prayed that Quin had made it out of the city safely.

The blast of hot air hit Lucius and Eprius seconds later; it was like being struck in the face by a scorching brick wall. It lifted both of them clear of the stones and high into the air. Burned, wind-battered and barely conscious, they crashed down close to the stone-covered surf.

After what seemed like many hours, Lucius blinked and opened his eyes. The stones beside him swayed and sloshed, and he thought at first that he must be dead and on the banks of the River Styx.* Gradually, it occurred to him that he was lying beside the sea – it was the waves that were moving the stones.

This had to mean that he was alive – he had survived!

The stones had stopped falling from the sky, and the world was filled with a hazy yellow light. Somewhere high above him, in the dust choked air, the sun was doing its best to shine.

It hurt him to move his head, even slightly, but he managed it eventually, and there, next to him, sat Eprius. His toga was in rags, his face dirty and his hair singed, but he was smiling.

'We made it, Lucius,' he said.

Eprius climbed tenderly to his feet, then put his hand out to help Lucius up. Eprius pointed to the southwest. 'What is that place?' he asked.

Lucius saw that the expanse of pumice continued as far as Stabiae, a wealthy resort on the coast. Beyond it

---

* *River Styx: in Greek and Roman mythology, a river which the dead must cross to reach the underworld.*

he could see crystal-clear blue sea, and, basking in the sunlight, the long arm of land that formed the southern end of the bay. Near the end of this promontory, he glimpsed the red-tiled roofs and white walls of a seaside town. It was towards this that Eprius was pointing.

'I think that must be Surrentum,' said Lucius.

'Shall we go?'

Lucius smiled and nodded. He put his arm around Eprius's shoulder, and the two boys began to limp their way along the shore.

END OF BOOK 2

FOLLOW LUCIUS'S FURTHER ADVENTURES IN:

GLADIATOR SCHOOL 3
BLOOD AND SAND

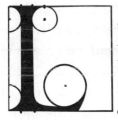ucius had spent the entire morning trying to coax an elephant to kneel before a statue of the emperor Titus. He was having no luck. He raised his *ankus* – a training stick as long as a man's arm – and slid it down the back of the great beast's foreleg, but the elephant remained stubbornly upright. She had knelt happily just a few minutes earlier and received a bucketful of tasty roots for her pains. But, for some reason, when faced with the square-jawed features of the most powerful man in the known world, she always opted to stand.

Personally, Lucius found it hard to blame the creature for refusing to show the man respect. After all, it was his imperial agents who had stolen her from her homeland in Africa and brought her here to this strange and frightening city. The elephant, so Lucius had been told, had been driven into a pit by Numidian hunters, then fed only barley juice for days to subdue her. In her weakened state, she had been transported in a shuttered cage across land and sea to the port of Ostia, then taken on a barge up the River Tiber to Rome. How terrifying must the crowded, noisy docks have seemed to this gentle animal reared in the tranquil expanses of the African plains?

Since then she had spent her days here at the vivarium in the Trans Tiberim* district of the city, on the western bank of the Tiber. She had been trained to do tricks – to throw spears in the air, stand on upturned buckets, and fight bulls. And she'd had to get used to a much more crowded and noisy world than her old home. Her enclosure was a cage of closely spaced bars, just ten paces to a side. It was one of hundreds of similar cages in the vivarium, containing beasts from across the empire. To the elephant, it must seem a loud, smelly and terribly alien place. Did she ever think about what she had lost – the forests, the muddy lakes, the wide open spaces, and the herd she had left behind?

Lucius checked himself. It was a fault in him to get sentimental about the animals in his care. He had even gone so far as to give some of them names. (He'd

---

* *vivarium: a place where live animals are kept and raised. Trans Tiberim: Across the Tiber; the area is called Trastevere in modern Italian.*

decided the elephant was called Magnentia.) He wished he could be more hard-hearted. After all, there were to be no happy endings for any of these beasts and he'd best get used to it. They had been brought here to Rome for one reason only: to perform, to fight and ultimately to die in the arena. In four days' time, the Inaugural Games of the Flavian Amphitheatre were due to begin. The night before, the animals of the Trans Tiberim Vivarium, and all the other vivaria dotted around the outskirts of the city, would be loaded into reinforced wagons and transported to underground vaults beneath the amphitheatre to await their debut in the show.

Lucius was about to give Magnentia another gentle prod when the door to the enclosure suddenly burst open. Silus, Lucius's boss, strode in. The beast master was a large, thickset man with a gleaming bald head, a thick beard and dark, angry eyes. As always, he clutched a coiled length of rope in his right hand – a bullwhip – ready to flick at any animal he felt like hurting at that particular moment. Silus enjoyed hurting animals – or so it seemed to Lucius. He used his whip randomly and without reason. He was violent, unpredictable, and all the animals were scared of him. As he came in, Magnentia trumpeted fearfully and bolted towards the far corner of the cage. In so doing, she knocked over the statue of Titus. It fell with a clatter to the floor and broke into half a dozen pieces.

'Stupid creature!' bawled Silus. He unfurled his whip and lashed her with it. The iron tip made a loud crack as it landed on her side. Magnentia bellowed with pain. He lashed her once again, and then a third time. Each time she roared her pain and tried to wedge herself further into the corner. Lucius cringed as he saw the dark red marks left on her skin.

Seemingly satisfied with the punishment he'd inflicted, Silus wiped the sweat from his brow, gathered up the whip and stuck it in his belt. 'The dumb brute has no idea how much it cost to get hold of that statue – nor what a crime she's just committed in breaking it.' He turned to Lucius. 'You, my lad, are going to have to repair it, even if it takes you the rest of the day. Understood? Have you got her to kneel before it yet?'

'Er… no, sir.'

Silus's nostrils flared impatiently. 'What in Jove's name is wrong with the animal? Those Numidians swore she was the most intelligent of the herd. And it's true she hurls weapons like no elephant we've ever had. And I've seen her kill two bulls with a single thrust of her ivories. So why won't she kneel?'

'She *does* kneel, sir,' said Lucius. 'Before you managed to find that statue, I'd get monkeys to crouch in front of her, and she'd kneel before them every time.'

'So she's prepared to submit to a monkey, but not to our emperor, is that what you're saying?' growled Silus. His hand moved to his whip – his automatic response to anything that annoyed him. 'Maybe she needs to learn the price of such disrespect…'

'No, sir,' pleaded Lucius. 'I think she's learned that lesson already today. Just give me a bit more time. I'm sure I can get her to do this.'

'We don't have much more time, boy,' snarled Silus. 'In four days' time, the emperor will appear on his podium at the opening ceremony of the games, and this elephant must kneel before him. This is my gift to him, and if she doesn't do as I demand, I will personally disembowel her with a blunt knife and turn her tusks into toothpicks. Understood?'

TO BE CONTINUED…

FIGHTERS IN THE

Secutor, 'the Chaser'
Weapons: gladius (short sword);
  dagger as back-up
Shield: large wooden rectangle
Helmet: full-face, smooth, egg-shaped.
Armour: padded or armoured guard
  on sword arm
Opponent: Retiarius; chasing the
  nimble Retiarius gives the Secutor
  his name

Eques, 'the Horseman'
Weapons: lance,
  short sword
Shield: circular cavalry shield
Helmet: with brim, and decorated
  with feathers
Armour: shoulder guard
Opponent: another Eques

GLADIATORIAL ARENA

Paegniarius, 'the Comedian'
Weapons: whip, wooden sword
Shield: small wooden board strapped
  to arm
Helmet: none
Armour: padded leg wrappings
Opponent: another Paegniarius; they
  are not serious fighters and always
  live to fight another day

Provocator, 'the Challenger'
Weapon: gladius
Shield: large, rectangular; superior
  version of legionary issue
Helmet: all-encompassing, with grille-
  covered eyeholes for visibility
Armour: protective sleeve, greave
  protecting the forward leg,
  chest protector
Opponent: another Provocator

A selected list of Scribo titles

The prices shown below are correct at the time of going to press. However, The Salariya Book Company reserves the right to show new retail prices on covers, which may differ from those previously advertised.

All Scribo and Salariya Book Company titles can be ordered from your local bookshop. Visit our website at:

www.salariya.com

They are also available by post from:

The Salariya Book Co. Ltd,
25 Marlborough Place
Brighton BN1 1UB

Postage and packing **free** in the United Kingdom